CHILD *of* GILEAD

DOUGLAS S. REED

The Hurricane Group

Printed in the United States of America
Library of Congress Control Number 2020910039

A record of deposit for this book is available from the
Bermuda National Library

ISBN 978-0-947481-87-2 (Paperback)
ISBN 978-0-947481-88-9 (e-Book edition)

Cover & Book Design by Danna Mathias

The Hurricane Group
2 Loyalty Drive
Somerset, Bermuda MA 01

ALSO BY DOUGLAS S. REED

Garden's Corner

For my younger brother, Kemet,
wherever you may be, always know this,
you are loved.

Religion that God our Father accepts as pure and faultless is this: to look after orphans and widows in their distress and to keep oneself from being polluted by the world.

—JAMES 1:27 (NIV)

If you think that you can only touch God by abandoning everything in this world, I doubt very much that you will touch God.

—THICH NHAT HANH,
GOING HOME: JESUS AND BUDDHA AS BROTHERS

Thus saith the LORD; for three transgressions of the children of Ammon, and for four, I will not turn away the punishment thereof; because they have ripped up the women with child of Gilead.

—AMOS 1:13 (KJV)

ONE

"Take the road less traveled, my son. Always. No exceptions." Sounds like the start of a fairy tale, or some sort of fable. Kind of like the ones they read to us in school. But it's really Mama's playful way of talking fancy. It's just her way of reminding me about her golden rule. Her law. And though they're words that Mama can't claim as her own, "They do," as she always tells me, "reveal a higher truth about what it takes to live a more meaningful and transcendent life."

"Most importantly," Mama is quick to add, "the Road Less Traveled is the true way, and will best keep a child away from harm and danger."

All this elegant talk beats Mama just saying, "Boy, just do as I say. Take the long way home. Never take the shortcut."

But taking the Road Less Traveled makes life a little more difficult. It means getting off the bus a stop early or riding in the last car of the train and walking out the station's back exit.

Both put me about four long blocks further from my home. A real pain. Mama doesn't care.

Perhaps that's because the path she prefers I take seems almost too good to be true. There are nice brownstone homes set along quiet, tree-lined streets. You pass my school and its peaceful playground. You never see any children playing there. Nor do you ever see a Mr. Lonely—that's a man with no family, no friends, no home—sleeping on one of the park's benches. There are a lot of churches along this path, too. Some are small storefront churches. Some are big and look like cathedrals, like the one Mama and I go to. Mama says, "Walk this way home and you'll know that God is in this place. You'll see all that you *need* to feel good about life—a nice home, a school nearby to enrich your mind, and an altar to worship at." Most importantly, Mama says, "There's peace and there's quiet along this path, so you can listen to God talk to you."

But The City is a kind of funny place. You can walk a few blocks and feel like you found a little piece of heaven. Yet, turn a corner and watch out! You're surrounded by...madness! That's what Mama calls the world outside the peace and quiet of the Road Less Traveled. She calls it... The Madness.

It's kind of hard to tell where the Road Less Traveled ends and The Madness begins, and vice-versa. The circular path of the Road Less Traveled flows into The Madness at opposite ends of a simple two-block cluster of small storefront businesses. Businesses like Chef and his Golden Sun take-out spot, and Injun Rah's pizza joint. The Madness is where you'll find brothers and sisters from the Dark Continent selling traditional garb at their fashion boutique. And not long ago, The Madness was where you'd find my grandpa's old candy shop. A sort of general store. I can't tell you much more, because I'm not allowed to go there. It's an old, battered corner store. It sits across the street from what had been, at one time, an old gangsta social club called Illusions. Illusions' window used to be black with its name written in script and in dripping blood red paint. But now it's a nail salon with a windowpane that is large and clear, so that when you look inside, you see a group of lady manicurists from the Far East at work. The Madness is the world. It's a place where you can find anything and everything you want. I think that is good.

But Mama says, "No, no, not so fast. Don't be fooled by those profiting amid The Madness." According to her, there's no nobility in always giving people what they want. "Drug dealers give people what they want. Does that make them noble?" That's Mama talking. I'm just a kid.

"Stay away from The Madness. Take the Road Less Traveled, my son. Always. No exceptions."

Mine is the story of a little boy who doesn't always listen to his mama.

CHAPTER

TWO

There's a light that shines dim but steady at the point where a smoothly-paved road leading out of town meets the ragged, rock-strewn path of the low country. It's a tiny speck of light, one that radiates from within a battered wooden shack store that stands alone and secure amid the vast darkness of an open field.

Inside, the Old Man stands behind a glass-encased counter filled with candy. He is lean and sinewy, robust and fit for a man in the early light of his sixties. He surveys his empty store with a keen eye, searching for anything he may have forgotten to do before closing. The Old Man sees that all is well.

But this is no ordinary closing for the night. He has made plans that will take him far from here. How long he'll be gone, even he can't say for sure. One week, two weeks, perhaps three. So, this pause to look around the shop one last time has more to do with reassuring himself that the people of this village will be ok. The Old Man hasn't told anyone of his leaving. He'll just up and go without notice; kind of like the way he seemingly appeared out of the blue ten years before. Cruising along this unpaved road, he spotted a group of children playing beside an old, abandoned shack, and the small, empty home behind it. This was the place the Old Man had been searching for.

It belongs to me.

In no time, the tiny home out back was tidied up and rebuilt and became the place he would call his own. And just as fast, he had a hand-painted sign in the doorway of the once-abandoned shack. It read simply: Hannah's.

No one needed to ask the man where he came from. The people of the village deemed him as one of them and embraced what he had to offer. A little country store set along an open dirt field—three miles from the center of town, and a quarter mile from the last cluster of ranch homes along the main road. For adults, it offers a welcome respite after a long day of work at the slaughterhouse. The Old Man always has a cooler full of cold drinks, and a group of picnic chairs out front for them to sit on after a day spent spilling the blood of lambs.

Still, only a handful of adults actually make their way to Hannah's on any given day. Perhaps they're scared off by the steady flow of children who, when they hear the Old Man ring the bell on the front porch of his store, seem to magically emerge from the thicket of trees just off on the horizon; many of them hopping across the stream that runs deep and forever steady out in the back of the little house. Leaping from one bank to the other, the children know that Hannah's is really their place. At first glance, the Old Man seems to have very little to offer them except a small assortment of candy and ice cream bars. But the children come because they are welcomed. The land around his small shop is their playground.

However, the time has come for the Old Man to tend to business up north in The City, a place where there's a million lights that shine higher and brighter than those here in this little village. There are answers to questions he's been waiting on for years. The time has come to seek them out.

THREE

You can tell a lot about grown-ups and what they think about kids just by the names that they give children. I know a kid named after a bottle of liquor—Ci-roc. And I know a kid named from a word plucked out of the dictionary— Omnipotent. Seriously. I'm not making this up. These are names of kids in my school. To have a name with no meaning is sad. It's like having no name at all.

The parents I've learned of in the Bible were different. They gave thought when naming their children. Ishmael… *God hears.* Jacob…*God protects.* Samuel… *Asked of God.* If your mom or dad gives you a name like that, there's no doubt that you're in store for big things. You know you have a purpose. As Pastor, from our church, says, "You know your destiny by the name your parents give you."

I don't think most kids today are in store for anything big with the names they've been given. They all seem to mean one thing only, 'God's little lost child'.

But Mama says that my name has meaning, that I'm named after someone who saved her life. So, my name has significance. Still, when you ask who is telling this story, I think I'll play like God and simply say, "*I am* is telling you this story." I kind of like that. You won't have power over me by knowing my name.

Mama and I live along the Road Less Traveled in a nice, neat, three-story high brownstone. It's just her and me in this big house that was passed down to us by her parents—my Grandma, who's retired and living back on a nice tropical island out there in the Sargasso Sea, and my Grandpa, who died shortly before I was born.

There's no daddy in my life so I can only tell you about life with Mama. And it's ok. I don't have any real complaints. Mama's a teacher. She doesn't work in the neighborhood school I go to, but she is close by. Mama used to teach art, but this past year she was asked to be a second-grade teacher. Life with a mom who's a teacher means I practically OD on education. I guess it's almost like having a preacher for a father—Jesus, Jesus all day long. With my mama, there's no idle time for idle thoughts. Everything is a teaching moment. But Mama is not like your typical teacher at school. She's not about cramming boring information and test-taking skills into your head; useless and uninspiring things that kids end up forgetting the very next day. Many times, Mama doesn't even ask questions. Instead, she waits for *you* to ask one. She waits to see how deeply you've been thinking about things. So, when we go to the movies to see something like *Charlie and The Chocolate Factory*, it's expected that I'll ask questions. Questions like, "Why do bad things happen to the children in this story?" and "Why did the boy's father deny his child something he really loved?" Mama is just trying to have me achieve some sort of wisdom. Mama says schools are not in the business of teaching wisdom, at least not in The City. They're just in the business of profiting off children by selling new programs and giving tests every year meant only to complicate learning and keep kids confused and dumb. She says schools have become a soulless factory where teachers have to justify the jobs of bean counters, people who make up silly methods to teach 2 + 2 = 4, and who talk about "data this and data that." And because this is how the powers that be want children to learn, Mama has taken it upon herself to help me seek a deeper understanding of the world. That's what a good parent is supposed to be... a teacher of wisdom. Still, it would be nice to sometime just be able to come out of a movie and ask, "So, where are we going for ice cream?" But with Mama, she finds a teaching moment out of a little movie... in the summer. That's kind of crazy.

Life with Mama also means reading a lot of books, which I actually kind of like to do. I just don't like having to write about them when I'm done. Mama makes me write some sort of summary, or character sketch, or even a new ending. Mama takes it easy on me with math. She'll never admit it to her friends at work, but she thinks math is overrated. The principal at her school would have a baby cow if she heard Mama say something like that. "Math is so important," is what most people say. But Mama mocks them and says, "You're right. You need math in order to hoard money, and to measure walls to keep people out. You need math in order to make and drop bombs. Wow, imagine a world without math." But her friends tell her that a whole lot of pain and suffering has been caused by words and ideas written on a page. Still, Mama tells them that stories—well-told stories—though they may not reveal facts like a history book, serve a higher purpose. They reveal life's ultimate truths. She believes stories are the best way to get children to learn what is most important in life—how to relate to and understand people. Good stories reveal how we're all connected. "Besides," she is quick to add, "where's the humanity in a bunch of numbers on a page, anyway?"

But my life is not all about school and education. It includes some work too. I have basic chores around the house, like helping take out the garbage and putting away the dishes in the dishwasher. I spend time helping Mama clean out the basement's studio apartment whenever it's vacant, like it is now. That's time spent scrubbing out the refrigerator and bundling up old newspapers and magazines Mama keeps down in the apartment. It's hard work and it's boring work. However, Mama says it's *important* work because we get to open our home to someone in need. Mama likes short-term rentals and she usually rents it out month-by-month to students from the art college down the street from us.

I need to keep it real… I don't feel the same way as Mama about opening our home. I just see it as strangers, one after another, coming to live with us. They're intruders in our space. And no matter how quiet a person may be, their life becomes part of your life. If I had any say in the matter, I would always keep it empty. I prefer it to be just me and Mama alone in this world.

FOUR

There's an 8:04 train that will take the Old Man to The City. That's what the schedule posted on the station's window reads. There is no one there to tell him otherwise. It's Saturday and the tiny log cabin ticket stand is closed for the weekend. There are no other travelers for the Old Man to confer with. And, as is so often the case with the Old Man, he is alone.

Not that he minds. He takes a seat on a small bench out front and he waits. The Old Man pulls out a switchblade, and repeatedly flicks the blade open and then closed again. He begins to carve his name on the wooden bench, but after a few carvings, the Old Man stops and flicks the blade closed. Instead, the Old Man begins to think about the long ride ahead—twelve, thirteen, perhaps as long as fourteen hours. Enough time to reflect on the life he once knew back in The City. More than enough time to think deeply on what it is he hopes to find upon his return.

The Old Man pulls out a small Air Mail envelope. He stares at it for a moment. The postage stamp of the Queen in the upper left-hand corner is starting to peel off. The Old Man gently rubs the stamp back down to its rightful place and takes the letter out of the envelope. He has read it many times before, and he does so again with eyes that reflect the same sense of anticipation as when it first arrived two days ago.

To My Soldier,
    I hope life is treating you well. You and I are probably the last of a dying breed that communicate solely through letters and cards. I like that we've not gone the way of the world.
    You've written me often, asking about the child. And each time, it has been met with a profound silence. You've wanted to see the little girl who is not so little anymore. That little girl we left behind in the madness; the little girl who chose to stay behind, perhaps waiting on a return we both know to be impossible. You've wanted to see for yourself how her life has turned out. You've wanted to know for a long time if we were right in the path that we chose for her.
    Go to her. And while there, share with anyone who doesn't know you and is foolish enough to confront you, let them learn, "Your kind does not win."

The Old Man slips the letter into the envelope without reading any further. He begins to think back upon a little girl, seven or eight years of age. She is dressed in a pink short-sleeved shirt and white shorts. She wears tiny pink sneakers with a unicorn on the side. The little girl sits behind the counter of her daddy's candy shop, humming a song. Crayons are scattered atop the counter. She is feverishly drawing away, lost in a world of her own creation.

For the Old Man, there is clarity that comes with this memory. He knows that this journey is about one thing only, and that's keeping a vow he made to himself long ago, *"No harm must ever come this little girl's way again."*

CHAPTER

FIVE

Mama rarely lets me go out into the world by myself. Mama's idea of independence is to allow me to walk over to the library once school is out. That's nothing. It's only one block away. And once I get there, I cannot leave. I have to wait for her to come and pick me up after work. Sometimes, if the moon and the stars are aligned just right, and the weather is nice, maybe, just maybe, she'll let me go to the corner bodega to pick up a loaf of bread or something. Sometimes, she'll have me drop off a pair of shoes at Pharaoh's. Pharaoh is a cobbler whose shop is a block and a half away from our home. It's along the Road Less Traveled. It's one of the few places I get to go to by myself. And the only reason Mama lets me go there is because she's kind of chummy with Pharaoh, the owner.

Mama won't admit this: she's a fearful person.

But it's summer, and school is done for the year. It's really beautiful outside. I'm willing to take the chance that Mama will set me free. And so, I decide that I'll plead with Mama to let me to go take my bike for a spin down the block. I'll beg Mama to give me five dollars to buy two slices of pizza and a soda. "Can I eat it there… Maybe I'll see some of my friends… I'm a big boy now… I just turned ten… Please, pretty please."

I'm expecting Mama to give me the same sad-eyed look she always does whenever I ask her to go outside on my own. It's that 'sad to see my baby growing up' look. Sometimes, I think it's about trying to catch her at the right moment.

I approach Mama's room. She's lying on her side in bed. It's almost noon, but she's still in her pajamas. Mama's eyes are closed, but she's not asleep. Mama seems deep in thought. I hate to disturb her. But I do.

"Mama, can I take my bike for a spin down the street to get a slice?"

Mama opens her eyes. But does she really see me? It's almost like she's looking past me, her mind elsewhere. Mama doesn't put up much of a fight, she just tells me, "Yes, yes, you can go. I'll be outside on the porch watching for you."

Who's this woman letting me spread my wings?

———

The pizza shop is only one and a half short blocks from our home. The owner of this pizzeria is an old, roly-poly Italian man who has been in the neighborhood forever. I don't even know his name. He just kind of comes and goes as he pleases. One week he'll open up at ten o'clock in the morning. The next week, his little shoebox of a pizzeria will open at noon. The shop is right across the street from my school, and he does a lot of his business when school is in. But when class is out for the summer, he likes to go see his people in the place he calls the Old Country. The owner has a laid-back attitude about his business. Mama says, "Money is not his master."

I ride up to the pizzeria and find the iron front gate has been drawn down. Perhaps I am early. After all, it is just noon. The streets are mad quiet except for Pharaoh, who has a hose out and is spraying mists of water along the side of the curb. Pharaoh's shoe repair shop is right next to the pizza joint. Pharaoh is nice. I like him. He sees me and smiles.

Pharaoh calls out to me, "He's away visiting family. He'll be gone another week." Then, with a little wave, he heads back inside his shop.

Suddenly, I hear bike tires screeching behind me. I turn around and see this boy from my school, Tum Tum. He's the only kid outside for miles around, and he has come out of nowhere. Tum Tum doesn't say 'hello'. He just nods 'What's up?' He's being real cool. Tum Tum sees that the shop is closed, and says, "You'll have to go to Injun Rah's instead."

I don't know about that. Injun Rah's Pizza is not along the Road Less Traveled. It's in a part of the neighborhood that Mama says is off-limits. It's located in The Madness. Any friend of mine would know this. But Tum Tum is no friend. We were in the same fifth grade class, but that's all. We didn't sit at the same table. We didn't stand near each other in line either. I was the second shortest boy in class, so I was near the front. But

Tum Tum was the last boy in line—almost a half foot taller than the kid in front of him and about fifty pounds heavier too. But what do you expect from somebody who is twelve years old? You're not supposed to be twelve and be in the fifth grade.

Tum Tum doesn't have many friends. He's on the quiet side. But it's not the shy kind of quiet. It's more like the sneaky kind of quiet. It's his eyes that give him away. Tum Tum has these cold eyes that are windows to a gangsta's soul. They're icy, brown eyes that are always sizing someone up. Always plotting to get over on someone. And whenever he's not churning a plot over in his head, then he's talking about getting his big brother on you. If Tum Tum loses a pencil on his own but thinks *you* took it, "I'm going to get my brother on you." Accidentally spill milk on him at lunch, "I'm going to get my brother on you."

And so everybody is not only scared of Tum Tum, but they are frightened of his big, bad brother—the big, bad wolf as well. However, no one has ever seen him. But that's because it's said he's always in and out of jail, even though they say he's only like twenty years old. It's also said that Tum Tum's brother has a deep, "smile now, cry later" scar that runs across the right side of his face from when some gangbangers rolled up on him a few years back. Tum Tum's brother goes by the name of Scarface.

I'm not afraid of Tum Tum or his brother Scarface. I tell him that going to Injun Rah's isn't happening, and that I don't want to get in trouble. Tum Tum pretends to be looking out for me and says, "Don't be such a baby. Nobody's going to know. I won't sell you out."

Tum Tum's pleading with me because he's unaware of a truth that only I know: Mama really hasn't allowed me to spread my wings. The pizza shop is so close to my house that Mama only has to walk five steps away from our home, and take a long, hard peek down the street to see what I'm up to. "Let's race over to Injun Rah's. Come on, kid." Tum Tum calls everyone 'kid'. I guess that's what you do when you're bigger and older than everyone else. "Last one there buys."

There's a part of me that knows I ought to listen to Mama more. There's a part of me that knows if I am to keep it real, Mama knows what's best. She knows a little something about the world. Why be out in The Madness having to deal with people like Tum Tum? I glance back in the direction of my home to see if perhaps Mama is looking this way, checking up on me. She's not. But I don't need Mama's protection. I can handle Tum Tum on my own. I tell him, "I'm not racing you. End of story."

"You're just scared you're going to lose."

"I'm not scared. I just know that you don't have money for slices if *you* lose."

"I got money. I've hidden it down on the side of my sock. Trust me, it's there."

That's hard to believe. Tum Tum's a Section 8 baby. Free breakfast, free lunch at school. The teacher pays his way on class trips. He never has money. I should feel a little sorry for him, but I don't. I never feel sorry for people who try to get over on me, no matter how poor they are. That's why I decide to tell Tum Tum, "OK... OK... you're on."

Tum Tum is slick. He takes off without giving me the chance to get back on my bike. Tum Tum darts down the main avenue. It's littered with so many cars that he'll have to ride on its bumpy sidewalks. That is going to slow him down. However, there is more than one way to get to Injun Rah's. I choose a side street with fewer cars and less traffic. At first look, it appears to be the longer way, but I can ride my bike down the middle of a nice, smooth street with no problem.

Tum Tum takes a peek over his shoulder. He realizes that I am not following him. He sees that I have chosen another path, and this surprises him. Tum Tum stops pedaling for a second and I can see this weird look on his face. A light suddenly goes off—he knows I have him.

I don't even pedal fast. The block I choose to ride down is so quiet. I pass my schoolyard—nobody is out there. An old, silver-haired lady is sweeping out in front of her carriage house. She stops sweeping for a moment and I can feel her eyes on me. She is watching me. I don't like being under some stranger's gaze. But I am not stressing it too much. I have a slice of pizza to win.

———⌣———

It's been a long time since I was last at Injun Rah's—with Mama, of course. Injun Rah's place has booths for you to sit in, and a large four-seat table in the middle of it all. Like the pizzeria I'm allowed to go to along the Road Less Traveled, it has that real strong smell of garlic, and sausages, and the pie-crust baking. And it hits you in the face the moment you enter, just like it does at the other spot. But something's not right.

Maybe it's because the owner is from the Land of Gandhi or perhaps the Navajo Nation. I don't know. People just call him Injun Rah. Kind of ignorant, I know. Mama says it's not right. She says he has a name. But Injun Rah never says anything. He's a short, string bean-sized man with a few limp strands of black hair atop his head. Injun Rah takes your order—or should I say 'your money'—with a smile. He's always smiling. Mama says it's because he's at peace. I think it's because he knows it's funny for someone like him, from the Land of Gandhi or Navajo Nation, to be selling pizza. Who knows?

What I do know for sure is that I am, who I am—and that's a winner. I have made it to Injun Rah's first. When Tum Tum finally does come racing into the shop, he is all out of breath. I know he is getting ready to sell out on the bet.

"No fair... no fair. My asthma."

I pay him no mind. I have no time for ghetto kids claiming asthma when all they are is out of shape. I make my way to the counter while Tum Tum trails behind me. "Come on, kid. Hook me up. My asthma... I had to stop... lost my money... it fell out of my sock."

Then a voice, harsh and deep, calls out from somewhere nearby. "Stop lyin'. You didn't have no money. You know you a broke nigga."

I look around and I see someone I've never seen before standing in the corner. He looks too old to be from the high school. He is light-skinned... real light-skinned. Probably somebody

Mama would call 'redbone'. He has cornrows that are neat and tight, and go way down to the back of his neck, almost to his shoulders. He has a thin goatee. The dude is smooth, sporting a baggy, bloodred polo shirt, and denim jean shorts.

"Wha… what's up, Fox," stutters Tum Tum.

"You ought to stop lying."

"Stop lying? About what?"

"You don't have asthma. And you know that you have no money."

"I was just playing."

Injun Rah approaches the counter with Fox's slice of pizza on a paper plate. Fox grabs it and starts eating quickly. Just before he heads out the shop, Fox turns his dark eyes on me and says, "I've been watching you, little man. I like how you don't let people get over on you." And with that, he is gone.

Tum Tum can't even look me in the eye. Tum Tum mutters something under his breath like, "Wait until my brother gets back home." It's brave talk. But I know the truth and the hurt behind the talk. Tum Tum is just shaken up because he got called out. Now, I begin to feel kind of sorry for him. I know that he really is broke, that he doesn't have the money. I shouldn't have raced him.

I give Injun Rah my order. He looks at me knowingly. Perhaps he remembers me from the times I've been in the shop with Mama. And if he remembers Mama, then I imagine he knows that my grandpa used to own the candy shop just a few doors down. All I know is that when I go to pay Injun Rah, he shakes his head.

"Put your money away," he says.

Maybe he feels bad for Tum Tum. I don't know. I don't ask. I just tell Injun Rah, "OK," and I ask him to cut one of my slices in half and put it on a separate plate. That is the most I am going to do for Tum Tum. At least I have one-and-a-half slices of pizza and a soda. And it's free. All is right with me.

Tum Tum and I eat in silence until near the end, when he asks me, "What are you going to say when your mom asks where you been?'"

I just shrug. I don't know what I am going to say. I don't like the idea of lying to Mama. I'm hoping she won't ask me. Hopefully, she'll just assume that I had a slice from the pizza shop I'm allowed to go to along the Road Less Traveled. I should be more concerned about something happening on the way back home. But I have faith. What's the point of going through life scared? I have to believe God's got my back. He won't let anything bad happen to me. I have to believe that I'll get back to my house without getting caught up in The Madness.

SIX

The Old Man stares out the train window. He keeps a steady gaze on a burnt-orange sun poised high and bright in the sky above. His thoughts drift and he hears a little girl ask, "Why do we dream, mama?"

The voice that follows is familiar—the voice of a mother willing to indulge an inquisitive child. The mother tells the little girl, "When people are awake, they're not so concerned with God. Therefore, in order to get our attention, He speaks to us through our dreams."

"But what about those who say they don't dream, mama? Doesn't God speak to them?"

"He can't speak to those who don't know Him."

What follows is quiet. The Old Man imagines the child being sent on her way. But the voice of the mother remains. She speaks almost in a whisper and seemingly to herself. "Such talk sounds silly...."

The Old Man interrupts her in his thought, *No, it's not silly talk. They are just safe and simple words used to explain away the unknowable. They're half-truths spoken in order to comfort a child or those who think like one. Why not tell her how it is written that God once spoke to men—all men—with great clarity.*

The Old Man hears the mother say, "…but she wouldn't understand a God that is now silent."

The mother says no more. Her voice no longer emerges from the radiant light just outside the train window. The Old Man thinks back on those times when he sat in the rear of the candy shop and listened to a mother shape a daughter's view of faith. The mother would glance his way and wait for him to offer an opinion, but the Old Man never did. A glance is not a question, nor an invite to share his truth, so he kept his beliefs to himself. But the Old Man can't help but wonder now what that little girl has grown up to deem the truth. He can't help but wonder if after all that has happened, is she a believer?

SEVEN

"A voice is heard in Ramah, weeping
and great mourning.... weeping for her
children and refusing to be comforted,
because they are no more."
—Matthew 2:18

Patient—real quiet-like— is how Mama sits on the front stoop of our home. She has a pad on her lap, and a few coloring pencils in one hand. Mama doesn't hear me ride up. How can she? Her head is down, and she is deep in thought, engrossed in whatever it is she is creating. I don't call out and disturb Mama. I simply lay my bike softly against the front gate and run up the steps to cuddle beside her.

I've made sure to come back by way of the Road Less Traveled, the path she expects me to take. I have no reason to believe that Mama thinks anything is off because when she looks up from her pad, her mood brightens and she manages to give me that warm, quiet smile of hers. She no longer seems as weary or as sad as she had looked earlier. I rest my head upon her shoulder and get a better look at what she is working on. She's sketched together some soft colors like powder blue and light green.

Mama leans over and gives me a kiss on my forehead. "So, the prodigal son returns."

Because Mama likes to talk with a little flavor, I don't always understand what she means, so I ask, "What's a prodigal son?"

"It's a son who's been out in the world and returns home to a warm greeting."

I say nothing. Maybe she *knows* where I've been. But I give nothing away. I just nod my head as though I understand.

"How was your lunch?"

"Fine." At least I'm not lying. My lunch was fine.

I watch Mama take out a velvet red pencil to use for her sketch. Mama is not one who draws portraits or a still life. She likes to do more weird stuff. Weird stuff that requires you to make up your own meaning as to what you are seeing. What I see is always something gentle, like her. Mama is tiny, like an angel. You see her face and notice right away these real delicate features. Not sharp or pointy, just fine and soft. Her skin is co-coa brown. Not nearly a mark on her except for a small, slight, discolored scar by her left jaw. She has jet-black hair that flows nearly down to the middle of her back. It's naturally curly. And Mama has these eyes—light brown eyes—with lashes that are long and soft and delicate like butterfly wings. But there's a faint, black scar on the bottom of her left eye, whose eyelid flutters gently every now and then all on its own. I have heard people say that Mama has cat eyes. Mysterious eyes hiding secrets. They're wrong. Her eyes are warm and caring. It's just that quiet people get accused of keeping secrets. And that's what my mama is—she's a quiet person. She gives thought to everything she says. Mama doesn't talk just for the sake of talking.

Mama finishes her little sketch and shows it to me. "Do you like it so far?"

Before I can even answer, a man's deep voice calls out, "Nice drawing, Pretty Lady."

Mama and I both look up. It's The Doctor. He's the neighborhood dentist who lives and works two houses down from us. And now Doc has stopped by our front gate. He's big and cuddly—he looks like a fat doughboy. The good doctor seems harmless because he is quick with a nice smile and polite words. Having known my grandparents, he acts really familiar with our family. That's why he calls my mama 'Pretty Lady' because that's the short version of what people around the neighborhood used to call my grandmother. They called her the 'Pretty Lady Dame'. Still, no matter how friendly and real familiar the Doc acts, he still looks at Mama kind of weird—like with an evil eye. The thing is, Doc would never come out and say what is truly in his heart—or his mind.

But I know what's up. You see, Mama's pretty. And since she is so pretty, we can be anywhere—walking along the Road Less Traveled or amid The Madness or just sitting right here on our front stoop—and all the men just stop and stare. Sometimes, they'll say a few kind words like The Doctor. But I know these men are not noticing her beautiful smile or the nice clothes she always wears. They look at other things. They see her slim waist. They whisper about her "killer ass". They gape at her firm chest. I don't like the way men stare at Mama. It's the hungry gaze of a wolf—a big, bad wolf.

But Mama knows how to tame the beast. She offers The Doctor a half-smile and acknowledges his compliment with a softly spoken, "Thank you." He still lingers by the gate for a moment. He says something about how Mama looks so much like her mother. He talks about how people used to shout out 'Pretty Lady' to her as well. He's made this small talk before, so I take Mama's hand and hold it tight, and then I sit closer to her. It's my way of telling Doc that she belongs to me.

The Doctor finally waves goodbye and continues on his way. I keep my eye on him until he turns into his gate, and disappears down into his basement office. Mama doesn't give the Doc much thought. She goes about her business of adding touches of pastel colors to her sketch. Thanks to Doc, Mama has forgotten that she was asking me what I think about her drawing. I would remind her, but she seems at peace finishing up her work and humming a song. I leave Mama alone.

⌒

Once upon a time, there was a wolf, and this wolf was all alone. All of the other wolves had been caught or killed or driven off. But this last wolf stayed. And he did all of the usual wolfish things. He lived in a cave high up in the hills. He raided the flock for an occasional stray sheep.

He would appear from time to time, late in the evening, on a trail from the fields running down to the village to frighten some milkmaid or herds boy coming home a little too late from the watch. And this gave rise to the stories of his great, gnarled, bloody teeth, and his wet, long, lolling tongue, and his fiery, red, hungry eyes... the wolf had quite a reputation in the village.

But that was not the worst of it. The most horrible thing of all, the thing that froze the souls of the old men, caused the red faces of the young people to blanche, and the heads of the children to go deep under bedcovers at night, was what the wolf would do from time to time in the cold, crackling air of the frosty-silver moon, high on the stark peak of the stony mountain near the village. He would sit up there and howl with the sound of a thousand midnights. Those who heard it, swore it was a sound that only a beast whose soul was tortured and lost forever could make. And it chilled to the marrow everyone who heard it... everyone, that is, except one person.

Right after dinner is the start of what Mama calls the Quiet Hour. For at least sixty minutes, Mama says the TV has to be off. She says I can play no video games nor can I listen to any music. No internet, either. It's just Mama and me, together in the living room. Sometimes, we're there talking about our day or about what's on our mind. But most of the time, we don't talk. We just sit in silence. Being quiet is not a problem for me. I like what Mama says about silence—that it connects you to God. She says God reveals His love through silence. You just have to be still and listen. And so, when the Quiet Hour arrives, Mama and I make sure not to fill the quiet with noise and empty talk.

Mama is sitting on the ledge of our huge windowsill, just staring out into the distance. Mama's tired now. Perhaps all that work we've been doing, cleaning up the basement apartment, has finally gotten to her. But Mama could also be a little sad. I can't really say for sure. Her moods seem to change so quickly these days.

But Mama soon breaks the quiet, and softly asks, "What book are you reading?"

I tell her *Wolf and Boy*.

"I notice that you like books about wolves. Didn't you just finish reading that Chinese folktale called *The Wolf's Ghost*?"

"Yes, I did."

"Why do you like wolf stories?"

I kind of shrug my shoulders. I don't really know what to say. But when you have a mom who's a teacher, saying, "I don't know" is not an option. So, I say, "Wolf stories are never boring."

"And what makes them never boring?'

"It's just interesting how in all these stories people never seem to understand the wolf."

"What don't they understand?"

"They don't understand that a wolf never needs to prove that he's not a beast. He is not ashamed of what he is."

"The wolf accepts the truth about itself?"

"Yes, that's what I like about the wolf."

"That's a lesson we can all learn from the wolf, always accept your true self. Always seek to know and understand who you truly are."

EIGHT

A soldier holds onto a quote during The War. It is stuffed deep inside the pocket of his jacket. It contains two simple lines, well-known and handwritten on a card that never crumbles, in ink that never seems to fade:

> *There is no hunting like the hunting of man, and those who have hunted armed men long enough and liked it, never care for anything else thereafter.*

The soldier likes to steal a look at the quote during moments of deep silence that come between assignments.

The soldier hears a voice calling out to him from somewhere in The Jungle's shadows. It's the voice of a friend, the boat pilot, who says, "You won't be able to hold onto that forever. You will have to give up being the hunter one day."

The soldier tells his friend, "You are wrong about that. No one can ever transcend who he is."

"So, you're defined by the label of hunter?" asks the boat pilot.

"I'm defined by my actions. I'm defined by what I do."

"Change what you do, then."

But the soldier knows that in The Jungle there's no turning away from one's true nature. You cannot change what you do. Not during war.

Yet, despite this truth, the friend says confidently, "I know I won't be a hunter forever. These journeys up and down The River will end one day. There will be no more need for warriors like us."

The friend tells the soldier that he will leave it all behind; he will return home and go into business for himself, no longer be a slave to the government or any other institution. He'll find some neighborhood store, take it over and live out his days in peace and quiet.

The soldier is amused by his friend's dream. "You're going to be a regular Candy Man."

"Yes. No more killing once I leave The Jungle."

"A far cry from this life now."

"You can come join me in that new life, when you're ready," says the friend. "My door will always be open for you."

At the end of The War, there is no home for the soldier to return to. No family who remembers him or knows who he is. So, the soldier pays a visit to the one who is now called the Candy Man. He travels north to The City to see if the promise still holds true. When he arrives at his friend's house, he finds a woman sitting on the front steps of his friend's home. She is quietly reading a book under the fading light of dusk. She is a beautiful woman, of soft, precise features made more pronounced by short, curly hair set under a red bandana. The pretty lady looks up at him with a gentle and pleasant gaze. Before he can ask if this is the home of his friend, she says, "I know who you are. Welcome home."

The pretty lady extends a hand and leads him inside her home. She offers him a seat at their dining room table, and she brings him a cold drink and a meal. She speaks to him about the new life available to him. They have been waiting. The small apartment downstairs in the basement will be his. And so will a job working at the shop.

The pretty lady goes on to say, "I know much about you. Don't feel ashamed about the things you and my husband did during The War. I don't judge. I just want you to feel at peace here."

And with a knowing glance and a mischievous smile, the pretty lady assures the soldier, "There is no need for hunters here."

———

The soldier tells the pretty lady that he won't have trouble finding the Candy Man's shop. Her directions are simple enough, "Stay along the path for a few blocks. Turn right. You can't miss it."

The soldier does as he is told. He finds the Candy Man's shop exactly where the pretty lady said he would, beyond a grand row of majestically-built brownstone homes that quickly fade into a chain of battered and bruised, white stone row houses. The Candy Man and his shop are found at that point where a quiet one-way street intersects with the noise and bustle of a two-lane avenue.

The Candy Man is out in front of his store with a broom in his hand. He is gently sweeping dirt and discarded papers to the side of the curb. The soldier barely recognizes his old friend. Perhaps it is the weight and the muscle he has lost. Maybe it's the way he is hunched over while sweeping that makes him look much older than he is. He looks weak. But when the Candy Man looks up and finally notices his friend, the truth is obvious to the soldier. It's his eyes; they're the eyes of the weary. They lack the fire and intensity of a fellow fighter. They are not the eyes of a hunter.

Still, the Candy Man smiles and walks over. He warmly embraces the soldier. "You've come home."

———◦———

The soldier follows the Candy Man into the shop. His friend closes the door behind them and locks it. He places a sign in the door window that reads: CLOSED — WILL RETURN IN TEN MINUTES.

"Money is not my master," says the Candy Man, with a smile. "I can close shop for a few minutes to catch up with an old friend."

The Candy Man offers the soldier a seat on the high stool behind the counter. "It's the best I can do for you."

The soldier smiles and acknowledges the offer in silence. He takes his seat and looks around the candy shop. It is an inviting place. The walls are brightly painted in shades of white and yellow. There's a glass encasement that runs nearly the length of the store. He peers through a glass smudged with the tiny fingerprints of small children who must lean against it as they gaze in wide-eyed wonder at the candy stocked inside. The soldier is himself amazed at the array of candy in different shapes and sizes. The soldier glances up and sees comic books and magazines hanging in bins against the walls. The Candy Man walks to the back of the store and opens up a brightly lit refrigerator and pulls out two bottles of soda pop—one orange, one cola. The soldier smiles when his friend extends the orange bottle to him.

"Here's to forgetting what we once were."

The two friends clink the necks of their bottles. They drink in silence. Finally, the soldier says to the Candy Man, "I had no home to return to. I had no place where they knew me… at least not those people who should."

"It doesn't matter. I'm just glad you took me at my word."

"You're a lucky man," says the soldier.

"You've met my Pretty Lady Dame."

"Yes. Like I said, 'You're a lucky man'."

"She's a blessing. Met her along a promenade overlooking the East River, not too long after I came back. I liked to go down there and look out onto the water. Alone. One day, she saw me and told me, "It's OK to smile."

"It began as simple as that?"

"Yes. She asked if she could have a seat on the same bench. And we just began to talk."

"What it is it about her that you value most?"

"She doesn't force me to talk about what I once was. She doesn't force me to talk about the things that happened in The Jungle."

"You get that enough from others."

"Yes, and I get weary of people asking, 'What was it like over there?'"

"What do you tell them?"

"I tell them, 'As long as you have your nice, comfortable life of indulgence with your big TVs blasting mindless shows, and your bellies full from eating three meals a day plus snacks; as long as you have gas for your cars… you can't ask me what is it like over there. You have no right to know'."

The soldier nods knowingly, "Ain't that the truth."

"And what's the burning question the world wants to know from you?'

"They ask me, 'How many people have you killed?'"

"And what do you say?"

"I tell them, 'That's between me and the dead'."

The Candy Man walks over and looks out the front door window. "I'm happy, my friend. But I'm tired, too. I'm not looking to fight anymore."

He motions for the soldier to come next to him. He points to a group of men hanging out on the other side of the street. There are in front of a social club called Illusions. "There are people who want this store. The neighborhood is changing.

There won't be a use for dirty pool halls and social clubs like Illusions. But the corner store, though, will always be a haven for the type of business they want to do. They talk about partnership and needing protection. But this store belongs to me. They have another thing coming if they think this will turn into some dope house."

"The Pretty Lady Dame knows about this?"

"Yes. She's not oblivious to the greed that exists in the world."

The soldier takes a long look outside, and then he turns to the Candy Man. "No more worries, my friend. I'm here now for you and your family."

NINE

Our church is a huge cathedral of once-white stone that's now slowly turning gray. It's only two blocks from where we live. Mama and I rarely miss service. We have to be out of town for that to happen. Or there has to be a blizzard. Or a tornado. Only something out of the ordinary like that can keep us away.

Sometimes, I think our going to church all the time has nothing to do with God and hearing the Word. I think it's more like we just don't want to seem lazy. We don't want to break a life routine. Whenever I take forever to get out of bed or when I beg to sleep in just this once, Mama is quick to say, "How is it going to look for us to miss church when it's just right down the street?"

And so, here we are, another Sunday at church. And today, they're talking about Mama.

Pastor is telling a story about a woman named Hannah— that's my mama's name. Pastor is young with a youthful spirit.

He is athletically built and is a man with a flair for large, dramatic gestures and expressions at the pulpit. It's easy for him to have my attention now because he is acting like he is all exasperated when he says my mama's name.

Pastor is getting the church riled up, "Say 'Aaaah' for me. Hannaaaah! She couldn't appreciate the blessing that God had bestowed on her. Aaaah!" Pastor reaches for a silk hanky from his finely-tailored suit, wipes the sweat from his brow, and says, "Hannah has a fretful spirit. She is in serious need of a pivot point."

That he's mentioning Mama's name is probably the only reason that I'm even remotely paying attention. I'm so comfortable. I'm resting my head on Mama's lap. I have soft, kinky hair that is now braided into long cornrow braids that go down the back of my neck. And Mama's gently fingering my braids and massaging my temples. I'm practically purring like a kitten. The Pastor's voice sounds so far off. But I hear enough, and so I know that he's really talking to the adults. I should be in the Sunday school for the kids.

But Mama lets me stay with her during the grown-up service. She says after being cooped up in school for five days, I don't need to spend even more time in a classroom. Mama is allowing me, a kid, the privilege of being around adults. I'm happy because the grown-up service has more life than the Sunday school program. I like the praise part at the beginning of the service because we get to sing. When the music's working, I'm there clapping my hands in the sanctuary and dancing. I forget that a half-hour before, I didn't even want to come to church. Praise time is party time. It's the best time. I imagine that's what heaven is like—one big party of singing, dancing, praising and glorifying God.

Lately, though, Mama's been kind of a party pooper. She'll stand like everybody and she'll clap her hands. But she doesn't really sing or dance. I guess the spirit doesn't move her to do anything more than to just stand and silently move her mouth to the words. I think Mama prefers the part when she can sit down and just listen to the pastor preach... especially when it seems like he's talking about her.

"Hannah reached a point where she was tired of doing the same thing over and over... she needed a pivot point..."

I lose track of where Pastor is in his sermon. But soon I hear him talking about how a person's pivot point begins with prayer. Pastor talks of how God's wonders are produced by prayer. He speaks about how a person's prayers may go on for many years before their life changes for the better. This seems to make Mama slow her soothing touch. She motions for me to sit up.

I can hear Pastor a little better now and what he's talking about doesn't seem to make much sense. To have your prayers go unanswered for so long, especially when you're a good person—a good person, say, like Mama—well, there's something not right about that. Where's the joy in receiving God's favor when you're old and busted?

I look up at Mama, who is sitting a little straighter and is leaning forward slightly. It's like she wants to ask him, *when will my pivot point come?*

"A Man of God interceded for Hannah and that was her pivot point..."

Pastor is talking about a priest who comforted and gave strength to Hannah at her pivot point. Mama leans back in her seat, kind of uninspired-like. I guess she's thinking, *that's why people come to church in the first place... so that men like the pastor, a Man of God, can comfort them and give them hope.* I don't think Mama has come to church for easy, obvious answers. It's really like getting no answer at all. Church is supposed to be the place where you learn The Truth.

Maybe Mama wants to hear a truth about going to God for and by yourself. Or maybe she wants a truth that speaks of a Man of God, who is not part of the church... perhaps somebody amid The Madness who could be a blessing.

Who knows? Religion and church stuff get kind of complicated.

———

There's a stranger, an Old Man, sitting on the steps of our home.

He's short and sort of skinny. The Old Man is dressed in faded jeans and a navy-blue windbreaker. He has a salt-and-pepper goatee that's nicely trimmed—looking kind of cool, kind of gangsta. He seems OK, except for a scary, kind of nasty, jagged scar by his right cheek. And the old man has eyes that are strong and steady. They grab hold of Mama and me, never letting us out of his sight.

The Old Man, this stranger, has a switchblade that he's using to slice an apple he's eating. He flips it and I can hear the click as it closes. He reaches for a large duffel bag set by his feet. He places the switchblade inside and then takes a small white hand

towel from the bag's side pocket. The Old Man wipes away a
bead of sweat trickling down from the top of his shiny, bald head.
Then, after neatly folding the towel and tucking it away in his
back pocket, the stranger finally says, "Good afternoon, princess."

"Good afternoon," Mama says, politely but kind of cautiously.

With mischief in his eyes, the Old Man then asks, "Do you
still know me?"

Without blinking, Mama studies the Old Man. Then real
cool-like, she says, "Of course. You're from the old candy shop.
You were friends with my father."

———

Mama needs to talk to the Old Man alone. I want to stay, but I
know better than to ask. Mama doesn't like the idea of me getting
too familiar with grown-ups. So, I make my way up the stairs to
the second floor. But I stop halfway and take a seat on the steps.
I lean forward and peek through the wooden banister. I'm being
nosy. The large sliding door to the living room is open enough
for me to spot the Old Man on our couch. Mama walks up to
him carrying drinks on a tray. She hands one to him and then
takes the other glass and walks over to her seat on the windowsill.
I watch them as they sit quietly, sipping on their iced teas.

Mama watches the Old Man take a long swig of his drink.
Finally, she says, "I remember how you would sit in the back
of the candy shop on your stool, just watching everything.
Sometimes, you would take a broom and sweep, but you never
said a word to anyone. Kids were afraid of you."

The Old Man laughs, "That's the way your father wanted it. He thought it would keep trouble away."

I know what's coming next—silence. Because whenever there's talk of Mama's father, something happens: a dead, life-less stare falls across my mama's face. Kind of like a mask of shame and disappointment. But Mama doesn't hide behind that veil for long. She eventually speaks up, although it's real quiet-like, "That was a long time ago."

It looks like the Old Man is going to rent out the apart-ment. I listen to Mama remind him of the rules about staying at our house: no smoking, no loud music, no pets. Pretty basic stuff like that. Mama doesn't ask him a whole lot of questions like she's done with other houseguests. I don't hear her ask him, "Where have you been?" or "Where do you plan to work?" or "Who else do you still know out here?" Mama is just accepting this man who she knows from the old days.

And the Old Man has no questions for her. They're getting re-acquainted without words. It's kind of weird. They sit there almost like it's the Quiet Hour. Mama waits for the Old Man to finish his drink, and then says, "Let me show you to your old apartment."

⁓

They called my grandfather the Candy Man.

He was an ex-soldier who, after The War, came to own a candy store in that place Mama now calls The Madness. He married a woman from the Island of the Sargasso Sea. Everybody called her the Pretty Lady Dame. The Candy Man didn't live all that long. He died a few months before I was born. Mama doesn't share many stories about her father. Mama only talks of how he was a quiet man. Strong. But she doesn't mean the diesel kind of strong because he wasn't a really big man. I can tell that for myself from the few pictures Mama has of him around the house. Rather, Mama says, Candy Man was strong because he knew his place in the world. He stayed in his lane. Kind of like knowing the path that you're supposed to be on and not letting anybody knock you off course. There's not more to share with you about the Candy Man. It is what it is.

I've gotten used to the mystery that Mama has allowed the Pretty Lady Dame and the Candy Man to become. I'm just grateful and lucky that they graced the earth. I don't know if much of who I am is because of my grandparents. But I can say that much of what I have is because of them. This house is theirs—paid in full. That means Mama can make life for me nice with the money she earns from her job. And then the money we get from tenants is just gravy.

Still, I guess you can say that not knowing much about my grandparents makes part of me a mystery too. All I know is that I'm the son of Hannah and a father unknown. Since that's not much, I can add that I'm the grandson of the Pretty Lady Dame and of a man they called the 'Candy Man', who owned a candy store in that place Mama calls 'The Madness'. Doesn't sound like much of a story.

TEN

Hannah stands quietly outside the Boy's bedroom and waits patiently for her son to fall asleep. It does not take long. Assured that the Boy is sleeping, Hannah walks downstairs to the room where she spends her Quiet Hour. She finds her seat on the windowsill's ledge and gazes out onto a starless night sky. Hannah thinks about the Old Man who has come back. She remembers how he had left ten years earlier, without so much as a goodbye. At the time, she didn't give his departure too much thought. It had been a time of change. Her father had died, and a little boy was about to be born.

And so years passed, and Hannah had never asked her mother, the Pretty Lady Dame, whatever became of him. Still, there were times when she thought of the Old Man, and of those days when he sat quietly and peacefully in the rear of the shop. He was their soldier, a protective spirit over the store.

Hannah remembers how the children of the neighborhood feared the soldier because he never smiled. But Hannah, the little girl, knew that was not so. The soldier had a smile that seemed reserved only for her. Hannah would see it during those times she would spend alone with him in the stillness of the candy shop's back room while her father or the Pretty Lady Dame tended to business out front. His smile was easy and always subtle. It was one, Hannah remembers, that had a feeling of kindness behind it.

Hannah thinks back upon the smile, and how she often sought to steal a conversation with the soldier before her mother or father finished their business out in the front of the shop.

Who are you? Where are you from?

Why does princess want to know?

Because to my friends and me, you're a mystery.

If I told you I'm not from this place, and I told you I'm from somewhere far away, would that satisfy you and your friends?

Then we'd ask, 'Don't you miss this place that's far away from here?'

Well, princess, I will tell you there's nothing for me to miss. I like where I am. But maybe I'll go back one day, to the place that's far from here and reclaim what's mine.

Hurry, tell me more...

But the soldier never did. The mother or father would rejoin them. Or someone would come into the shop to buy something. The soldier would go back to what he was doing, cleaning or restocking the back room. Or he would simply return to sitting on his stool and watching over the store. Hannah would no longer hear him call her princess. He would call her 'Hannah', if he called her anything at all. And the little game they played would be over too. No more asking questions that were never answered. The truth would remain outside her grasp.

Hannah can't help but smile to herself. Not much has changed over the years. The Old Man is still a mystery to her, but he has returned, bringing a veil of solace and protection that is comforting to her.

And Hannah knows—that this is good.

ELEVEN

Curtains dance by an open window and awaken me from sleep. It is still early, but I am eager to get out of bed and do what it is all us children like to do—watch the bizarre and secretive doings of grown people.

The house is silent. I walk up to Mama's room. The door is open, so I glance inside. Mama doesn't move. She is fast asleep. I make my way downstairs.

In the kitchen, there's a battered door. It opens to a narrow set of creaky stairs that lead down to the ground floor. At the bottom of the steps, I can see the slender hallway and the door to the Old Man's apartment. I sit there at the top stairwell in the shadows, staring at his door. I hear voices coming from his apartment, so I take a step or two further down the stairs. The door to the apartment slowly opens and the Old Man slips into its crack. He studies me with those fierce eyes of his. "Come here," he says.

I do as I am told and walk to the bottom of the steps. The Old Man peers down at me and asks, "What are you looking for?"

"I thought I heard voices."

The Old Man pushes open the door just a little more. "It's just the TV."

He says it like it's something I should have known. The Old Man opens the door a little wider and I see that it is indeed the TV. He's watching the news. On the screen, I see a story about people wildin' in some country far away from here. There's news about bombs being dropped. There's news of destruction to people's homes and buildings. They show bloodied children laid out in the hospital, crying for their mamas. There are no images of any soldiers dying, just those of innocent kids getting hurt.

I point to the TV screen and ask the Old Man, "What are they fighting about?"

The Old Man doesn't say anything right away. I guess there's no easy answer, so he takes his time to respond. But finally, he says, "Well, one side believes they are protecting their people from terror. The other side thinks they're rightfully fighting a country that's been oppressing them for years. However, they're really battling about something else."

"What's that?"

"They're fighting over whose God is more powerful."

The Old Man is confusing me, so I ask, "Isn't there just one God?"

"That's what people believe. But religion has come down to being nothing more than a fight for people to prove 'My God is better than your God'."

"I don't understand. Why would people be fighting about God? That doesn't make sense."

"They're fighting because they've forgotten what the purpose of religion is."

"Which is?"

"To help people to understand."

"That's it? Religion is meant to help people understand. Understand what?"

"It's meant to help us understand why we are here. To help us understand our destiny. But there are a lot of different religions, each believing they have the one true answer to that simple question—'why are we here?' So, people fight to impose their views on everyone else."

"What's wrong with there being different paths that get you to the same place... to God?"

"Any grown-up who says that is speaking as a child. They're taking a position that's simply meant not to offend. They know there is really only one truth, but no one knows what it is. So they talk of many paths. But you know, even if there were many paths, the question still remains: who is God?"

"It sounds so confusing, even a little scary."

"Life is like that at times." The Old Man nods in the direction of the steps. "You should go back upstairs. You don't need to concern yourself with such thoughts. You're just a child. Just know that your mama will work hard to never let anything bad happen to you. She lives to protect you from the bad things of this world."

TWELVE

The Old Man sends the Boy on his way. He watches the child ascend the stairs and step into the light of an open door. The Boy disappears, leaving the Old Man to fix his stare on the darkness that has returned to the passageway. He hears a woman's voice call out to him.

"You are capable of doing what I ask?"

The Pretty Lady Dame appears, sitting atop the same steps in the shadows.

"I've said it many times before, . You can't transcend who you are."

"So, if you're a victim, you'll always be a victim? Poor? Disenfranchised? There's no hope for you? You're forever assigned that role?"

"I talk of my true nature. I speak of the things I do that make me who I am. I talk of acknowledging that part of man's nature that allows him to hunt, to kill even. You, though, speak of labels. You talk of the roles people allow themselves to be assigned by others. The essence of who you are does not come down to a label placed upon you by others. It does not come down to their single-word definition of you. But I suppose if you go through life accepting their labels and go through life acting poor and disenfranchised, if you always act like a victim, like you're the sheep, then that is, in truth, who you are."

"This is not a family of victims. This is not a family of sheep. That is why I come to you."

"What about forgiveness. Are you not capable of it? Doesn't your religion teach you that?"

"My religion teaches me many things. But I only honor those things that satisfy my aims. Not the things that do not. Let my enemies go to the Candy Man for love and forgiveness. That is what he believes in."

"And that is a sign of weakness?"

"Yes. I want someone strong who can put the fear of God in evil men. I want them to get on their knees and beg for their lives. Then I want them to know that their kind don't win."

"So, you can live with the thing you're asking me to do?'"

"Yes. But you still haven't answered whether or not you will do what it is I am asking."

"As I've told you before, I am the hunter. This is who I am. And so, I will do what you've asked."

Nothing more is said. The Pretty Lady Dame vanishes, and all that remains is Old Man and the truth of why he has returned to The City. "I will confront evil men who dare to cross my path and teach them—'their kind do not win'."

THIRTEEN

The Pretty Lady Dame lives in exile. There's no other way to put it.

Pretty Lady Dame left the City shortly after I was born, and never returned. Rarely do we speak by the phone, and never do we stay in touch by email. We simply communicate through words written on a page, usually a little note in a card. If it takes a couple of months between letters, so be it. The Pretty Lady Dame is old-school like that.

Normally, I don't have much to say. And neither does the Pretty Lady Dame. It seems as though we write to each other out of courtesy. Like we're playing the roles assigned to us in a movie—the attentive grandmom and the dutiful grandson. The Pretty Lady Dame will write and ask the usual stuff, "How is my little warrior doing?" or "Are you behaving yourself?" I write back telling her that all's good, and that, of course, I've been on my best behavior. I'll tell her a little bit about school.

Pretty Lady Dame ends every note telling me that she misses me and that she can't wait to see me again.

But there's no telling when that will be. Mama and I don't take a yearly vacation to see her. I have only spent time with the Pretty Lady Dame on one occasion, and that was three years ago, when I was seven. It was summer and Mama took me to visit her. The Pretty Lady Dame lives on a tiny island out there in the Sargasso Sea. It is always hot, and it is clean. It is pure— like a little piece of heaven on Earth. There's not much to do out there, but that's OK. My routine that summer was this: wake up late, eat lunch, go to the beach, come home, eat dinner, go to bed, wake up late, eat lunch… you get the picture.

It's not a bad life because the people are friendly and the beaches are so beautiful, with crystal, clear blue waters and pink sands. And the Pretty Lady Dame lives in a small pink cottage with a white roof that overlooks the sea. The view from the Lady Dame's home is spectacular. I remember there were many days when I would sit alone with the Pretty Lady Dame, just gazing out to the ocean. She'd never sit beside me, always just slightly behind, and over my left shoulder. We wouldn't say much. We'd just soak up the beauty of it all. Most days, the turquoise water was calm, and I'd sit there alongside the Pretty Lady Dame watching the waves gently breaking against the outer reefs that dot the coastline. But some days, the sea would look furious, and you could no longer see the reefs because the white caps from the waves hid them. One day I said to the Pretty Lady Dame, "Why does the sea seem so angry?"

The Pretty Lady Dame said nothing. She didn't offer up an opinion of her own. I assumed she hadn't heard me. The Pretty Lady Dame is a woman of few words. That is something I came to learn during that visit. Often times, we'd sit in silence when she drove us across the island or when we sat around the dinner table, just she, Mama and me. So not hearing her speak right away didn't surprise me. But she was sitting so close that I knew she had to have heard me. And there was something about the silence that was too long and awkward. Almost like she was refusing to acknowledge me. So, I glanced over my shoulder, and I could see that she was looking my way. The Pretty Lady Dame was staring through me with that look—the same one I see in Mama whenever she talks about her father. It's a look that I've come to fear because it's a look devoid of love. It's all disapproval. If I was brave, I would have asked, "Why do you look at me that way? What have I done for you to look at me with such venom?" But I didn't ask. I don't want to live with a truth that tells me my own blood hates me. I'd rather live with my own truth. So, I told myself that the Pretty Lady Dame had something else on her mind. I didn't ask the question again. I just let the moment go and let the question fade away

I take out a notepad from my desk and begin jotting a few lines to send to Pretty Lady Dame.

> *Dear Pretty Lady Dame,*
> *How are you? Mama and I are good. School is over*
> *for the summer. I'm happy about that. Things could*
> *be interesting this summer. A man has come to visit.*

He is a friend to you. Do you know why he has come?
Mama seems happy he has come here. Anybody who
makes Mama smile can't be bad, right...

———

I ride my bike by Mama's side. We are on our way to the market.
We come upon my school's playground. I stop my bike, and I
ask, "Can I go to the playground while you're in the store?"

Mama's eyes begin to narrow, and she takes a hard look over
at the playground. The supermarket is only across the street—
like a hundred yards away. I want to tell Mama that I'm grown.
That I'm getting to that age when she has to stop babying me.
Though her hard stare never brightens, she says, "You can go.
I'll be inside for only a few minutes."

———

There's a little girl alone by the swing set. I didn't notice her
when I first asked Mama about coming to the playground, but
she is here now. I don't know who she is, but I'd say she is a
grade or two below me. She's a sweet-looking girl, the color
of milk chocolate. Her black hair is pulled back into one long
braid, and she has eyes—brown, and almond shaped—that
have a way of hypnotizing you. She also has a cute, little button
nose. I think I'll call her 'Pretty Girl'.

Pretty Girl's dressed in a pink top and a pair of green shorts.
On her feet are plain, all-white sneakers. I notice she's wearing a

gold engraved anklet with fine diamonds. It's a little too big for her, and so it hangs loosely on her ankle. There are two words written in script that is hard to make out. Still, it looks kind of nice even though I've never seen a girl so young wear one before.

Pretty Girl is not swinging very high. And she doesn't seem to care either that she's hardly moving. I ask her, "Do you want me to give you a push?" Pretty Girl nods OK.

So, I push. And as I do, she keeps going higher and higher. I hop on my swing and I get it going until I catch up to Pretty Girl and we're swinging in unison. Pretty Girl glances over and smiles. But all of a sudden, she lets her swing come to a stop and runs away. I leap off my swing and chase after her.

"Why are you leaving?"

Pretty Girl points towards a man standing by the front gate. He is mad tall and is as skinny as a toothpick. The Thin Man. I can barely see a slender face hidden under his baseball cap. I ask Pretty Girl if that's her father.

She says nothing. Maybe she can't be seen talking to boys. But I still have to ask her something. "Hey, what's your name?"

Pretty Girl just smiles, and then says, "Why do you ask me my name?

I tell her, "Because I don't know you."

Pretty Girl just smiles and skips away without saying anything. The Thin Man begins walking. Pretty Girl catches up to him and takes him by the hand. She and the Thin Man soon disappear out of sight.

I go back to the swings to pick up my bike. There's no one else in the park for me to play with, so I figure I might as well head on over to the supermarket and wait for Mama there. But it turns out, I'm not alone.

———

The Old Man is sitting on a wooden bench on the other side of the playground fence. He is looking at me with those intense eyes of his. The Old Man has on this crisp, red silk shirt. He's still wearing jeans and his Tim's. The Old Man has on a blue baseball cap.

When I ride up to him, the Old Man asks me, "How are you?"

"I'm good."

He tells me that he was out for a little walk, but he stopped when he saw I was alone in the playground. He wanted to make sure that everything was all right.

"Mama said it was ok for me to play in the park while she shops. She's only going to be a few minutes. You didn't have to worry."

The Old Man begins a slow walk, and I start to ride alongside him. He is seemingly headed in the direction of The Madness, probably to see what's become of the Candy Man's shop.

I ask the Old Man if he's on a walk to see how much the old neighborhood has changed from when he and my granddad were friends.

"I guess you can say that."

"What did you and my granddad do together?"

The Old Man doesn't answer right away. He begins to laugh, almost to himself. Then he says, "We did what all good friends do together—have fun. Well, as much fun as war allows."

I want to tell the Old Man that I wouldn't know about that. I don't really have friends. I only know some people and some people know me. But I don't want to seem like Kid Lonely, so I say nothing. I prefer to stay on the subject of my grandfather, so I ask, "Were you and my granddad friends before The War—like friends in school?"

"We don't go back that far. Met your granddad during The War, and then worked with him afterwards."

"Doing what?"

"Like your mom said, I'd sit in the back of the store and just watch out for things."

"Didn't you get bored?"

"Being mindful of things around you... spending time thinking deeply on things... is never boring."

We are getting closer to The Madness. You can always tell because you hear music booming from speakers perched on the sills of open windows. Wild, shirtless children, with no mamas or papas around to look after them, are darting between parked cars, playing tag. Half-naked bodies sit on open windowsills, looking out onto the action happening down in the street below. I tell the Old Man that I can't go any further. I have to go back. Mama is expecting me.

"Little boys should always do as they're told. Your mom knows what's best for you."

The Old Man nods in the direction of the park. He is sending me on my way. I pedal a short distance and stop. I watch the Old Man vanish into The Madness. As for myself, I turn around and head on back down the road I'm supposed to go down.

FOURTEEN

"*Wisdom will save you from the
ways of wicked men.*"
—Proverbs 2:12

The Old Man steps off the path that leads to the old candy shop, and finds himself on a quiet and lonely block. On one side of the street is a large, pebble-strewn lot, where a handful of cars sit parked behind a wire fence with a locked-gate. The lot sits next to a vacant warehouse that takes up the other half of the block. Across the street, where the Old Man now walks, is a small bread factory. It's a nameless, red, brick building, three-stories high, where the sweet aroma of fresh baked bread floats out of large open windows on the second floor. Next to the bread factory, near the block's end, is a print shop.

It is a small, narrow space, obscured by the bread factory on one side and a storefront church on the other. On display in each corner of the print shop's dingy window are silkscreened T-shirts promoting neighborhood youth leagues, restaurants, and salons. Immaculately printed brochures, pamphlets, and glossy cards are spread out neatly on a ledge at the base of the window. This is the place the Old Man is looking for. Without hesitation, he steps inside.

The Old Man walks up to a chest-high counter where a sweet and studious looking young woman in frameless glasses sits. She has flawless, deep chocolate brown skin, and is neatly dressed in jeans and a gray T-shirt with the shop's name printed on its front. The young woman is studying a stack of invoices. Behind her, three machines shake, rattle, and roar as they spew out copies at different speeds. The Old Man approaches and taps the counter to get the pretty woman's attention. She looks up at the Old Man with innocent, yet playful eyes. The young lady greets him with a welcoming and pleasant smile. "I'm sorry; I didn't hear you come in."

The Old Man nods. He waits for her to say more.

"May I help you?"

The Old Man studies the beautiful young woman for a moment, and then he asks, "Do you know me?"

The young lady smiles softly. She unfastens the lock to the counter's small door and swings it open. The Old Man passes through. The young lady leads him past stacks of boxes and three tall shelves filled with reams of paper. The Old Man is led to a locked door in the rear of the shop. There is a buzzer that the young lady presses twice. The door opens slightly on its own. There are steps leading to the basement. The pretty young lady tells the Old Man, "You know the way."

The basement is dark. The main source of light comes from a row of computer monitors set along the bank of a long, wooden table. A smallish man in wrinkled, button-down white shirt and tan slacks sits at a small wooden desk. Underneath the muted glow of small lamp, he looks through a magnifying glass at a passport book. He takes out a pair of tweezers, and with his tiny hands, begins to adjust a photograph that he is trying to set properly. Old Man waits for him to finish. The small man finally looks up from his work. "My friend, please." The small man motions for the Old Man to come near.

"I wasn't sure I could still gain entry," says the Old Man, with a smile.

The small man laughs quietly before responding. "Knowing the right question and its answer always will." He begins to clear off his desk, putting a handful of passport books and photos into a folder.

"I see that your daughter is working the front, and not your wife."

"It was time for her to learn the family business. I don't want her to have any delusions about her poppa. I help people in need of a new identity. No questions asked. There's no sin in letting people start a new life with a new name. It's better that my child knows the truth about me. Less likely that harm will come her way."

There is an awkward silence. The small man opens a desk drawer and places the folder inside. "I wasn't expecting to see you again. Unfinished business for you and the Pretty Lady Dame?"

The Old Man doesn't respond in words—he affirms with a knowing glance.

"Still seeking out people who must learn the lesson… 'your kind don't win'." And though the small man is pleased that he knows his friend's purpose, there is more that he feels is unanswered. "But why come see me? You don't need my kind of help again."

"I wanted to hear from someone who might know: is it safe to be back?"

"A lot of time has passed since you and the Pretty Lady Dame went away. The neighborhood is changing. All the shop owners used to know each other. We were like family. We would do anything to protect one another and our families. But only a few of us remain… Injun Rah… Chef… Pharaoh. I couldn't tell you what's going on at the old shop. I stay off the radar. I stay here, underground, out of other people's business."

"That's not an answer."

"No, it's not, because 'is it safe?' is not the right question."

The Old Man studies his friend for a moment. "OK, then. Is my mark still there?"

"I think we both know the answer to that question. My friend, that is something you're going to have to find out for yourself."

The old candy shop sits on the corner where the Road Less Traveled meets The Madness. It's a nondescript storefront of red brick, saddled up next to a liquor store. The front window is covered with dog-eared posters of half-naked women advertising malt liquor. The posters obscure whatever business is being done inside.

The Old Man approaches the store. Standing in the shop's doorway is a sly young man with dark, sullen eyes. The Old Man sees a kid with too much time on his hands—a young man from a lost generation—leaning against the doorframe and blocking his path into the store. The young gatekeeper is long, and sinewy, and projects an aura of menace. He speaks to the Old Man in a voice harsh and dismissive of the elder standing before him. "What can I do for you, pops?"

The Old Man is unmoved by the young man's intimidating tone. The Old Man thinks to himself, *he is just a boy; he doesn't know me.* The Old Man deliberately let's silence slip in the space between them, before he eventually answers. "You can start by not calling me 'pops'."

The young gatekeeper knows an older generation that is fearful of its youth—adults who are weak and unwilling to fight back against a child's challenge to their authority. But the Old Man has made a child blink. The youngster is unsettled and shifts his weight ever so slightly. His lean against the door has now straightened. To feign disinterest, he takes a bloodred handkerchief from his back pocket and wipes his brow. "Anything else?"

"Then you're going to move out of my way and let me pass."

The young man's eyes narrow, and he takes a step closer to the Old Man. But then a voice calls out from the back of the shop. "Fox, move away from the door."

The Old Man takes one step inside and his eyes search out for where the voice has come from. He sees a Merchant. He's a black man, the color of night. The squat, sturdy middle-aged man stands by the door that leads to a back room. There are shadows moving in the room behind him. However, the Merchant turns his attention, and a pair of dangerous gray eyes, on the Old Man.

"Can I help you?

"Just looking to buy a newspaper."

"There are no newspapers here."

The Old Man takes a long glance around the shop. Gone is the finger-smudged glass encasement that the neighborhood children used to press against in wide-eyed wonder at all the candy stocked inside. Comic books and magazines no longer hang in bins against the walls. Instead, the old candy shop is home for coolers barely filled with bottled soda and beer. The store has become dank and spare, with two shelves in the center of the shop, sparsely stocked with a few basic canned goods and bread. The Old Man's curiosity has been met. He tells the Merchant. "Thank you. That's all I needed to know."

The Old Man goes on his way past the young gatekeeper. The Merchant comes from the back of the shop and stands next to Fox. Together, they watch the Old Man walk away.

Then the Merchant turns to the young man named Fox, and says, "There's something I need you to do."

FIFTEEN

Mama has a studio up on the third floor of our home. It's an open space where she keeps a bundle of canvasses. Unfinished work is tucked away in a corner and covered by a paint-splattered tarp. Large portfolios are neatly stacked around an easel that sits propped up in the center of the room. Another blotchy linen sheet lies across the floor, and flattened tubes of paint lay scattered at the easel's base. Mama's studio shows that she's serious about her art, but the truth remains, none of her work ever leaves this room. This studio is really a place to keep her art hidden from the world.

And it is a sanctuary too. It's another place for her to spend some quiet time—alone.

Mama is there now, sitting in a darkened corner.

She can't see me peeking around the edge of an open door. Sometimes, the only way to understand Mama and her ways, is to watch her from a distance. It's really the only way to see if Mama is keeping secrets. I think she is.

I watch her pull out a black portfolio book from behind the easel. Mama begins to flip through it. She pauses a few pages in. Mama's found what she is looking for. There's no real expression on her face. Whatever it is she's looking at, doesn't seem to bring her any joy. Mama just looks at the page for a real long time, while she gently traces her slender fingers across the paper. Mama is slipping into a sad place.

I want to run up to her and say something that might make her happy. That would make *me* feel good. But it's not about doing something that would make me feel better. So, I leave Mama alone. Sometimes, the best thing you can do for a person is to just be silent.

I stop spying on Mama. I leave her in peace.

—⁓—

Sometimes, when I sit outside on the front stoop of my home, it gets so quiet that it seems as though I'm the only kid around. The quiet is that deep. It makes me feel sad. It makes me feel lonely. Come to my peaceful block—by way of the Road Less Traveled, passing my school and its empty playground—and I'm sure you'll ask yourself, "where have all the children gone?"

There are times when I can't help but think adults are up to something shady. It's as though they're doing foul things to children. It's like they're hiding them away and silencing them. Even Mama has abandoned me to deal with her darkened mood. I've been left alone to keep myself company on the front stoop with a book in my lap.

But a man appears. He is standing by our front gate and he's watching me. But I'm not afraid because I know this man. He's from my church. It's Pastor. His smile is always bright and welcoming. Pastor looks smart. If I didn't know who he was, I'd say he kind of looks like a teacher with his narrow, black, framed glasses and simple clothes—a regular, old, blue button-down shirt, some beige khaki pants, and loafers. The Pastor is clean-cut. Obviously, there's nothing gangsta about him.

I'm ok with the Pastor because he doesn't give me the creeps like the other men who try to talk to Mama. The Pastor is harmless because he's religious. Of course, he's full of the Lord. Everything is about God, and Jesus, and blessings. That's what you'd expect from someone like him. I guess that's not so bad. There are worse ways to be. After each Sunday service, if we see him, he'll tell us to have a blessed week. He's the kind of guy around whom you feel the need to act perfect.

That's why I straighten up before saying to him, "Good afternoon." I don't say my usual, "What's up?"

The Pastor smiles at me, and asks, "Are you enjoying this blessed day?"

I tell him, "Yes, Sir."

As nice a man as he is, there's still a part of me that can't help but wonder if Pastor would greet me and bless me, if he didn't want to talk to Mama... if I was just some lonely kid... a lost kid. He is just a man of flesh and blood. He's not perfect.

Still, I shouldn't question his niceness. I should be more perfect. So, I ask Pastor, "How are you doing?"

He gives me a "full-of-the-Lord" type response that makes some people roll their eyes. He says, "I'm feeling blessed and highly favored." I don't give such talk much thought. It is what it is. He's in love with God. So be it. I listen as he tells me how he's on his way back to the church. Pastor asks me if I'll be attending the church's summer camp again this year. I tell him that I'm not. Mama didn't sign me up.

"How is your mom?"

"She's fine. She's upstairs in her studio."

"Ah, working on her art."

I should tell him the truth, that's she's lost in thought with some old portfolio. But I let what he says go unanswered. Even though he might be able to help her, I don't tell Pastor about Mama and her sadness. But his smile remains bright. Mama's unseen presence is enough for him. That I can speak on her behalf, satisfies him. He tells me, "You have a blessed day."

Pastor leaves, and as soon as he does, the gate to the basement apartment slowly swings open. It's the Old Man. He steps outside and looks up at me. "Everything all right?" He looks off in the direction of where Pastor is headed. "Was that a stranger?"

I assure him that the voice he heard was not that of a stranger. I tell the Old Man that it was the voice of someone I know. I tell him that it's the pastor from our church.

The Old Man nods respectfully, but still asks, "So, you're alright?"

"I'm good." I feel as though I can talk like my regular self around the Old Man.

The Old Man seems satisfied. He sees the book in my lap, and asks, "What are you reading?"

I tell the Old Man, "*Wolf and Boy.*" And then I ask him, "Do you like to read?"

"My eyes don't work as well as they used to, but I like to hear a good story. Tell me about the one you're reading."

There's not much to tell the Old Man, I just started reading *Wolf and Boy.* Still, I tell him about what I've read so far. I tell him it's a story about a wolf that has brought fear to a village. How everyone lived in fear of this wolf except for one person… a boy.

"Perhaps you can read me your story. You'll be my personal storyteller."

He takes a five-dollar bill from his pocket. He leans forward, and in a hushed voice, says, "A little something for each day that you read to me."

"You don't have to pay me. Mama wouldn't like that."

"Our little secret."

I take the money and put it in my pocket. It's just a little something to help buy ice cream when the truck comes around. There's no harm in that. Besides, we all have secrets. Mama has hers. Now I have mine.

"So, read on," says the Old Man. "Tell me more of this story, *Wolf and Boy.*"

Living in the village was a boy, who had lived there all of his life. And yet no one really knew this boy. I mean, he spoke to folks, and they spoke to him. But no one really understood him or cared to. Even his parents were at a loss to understand his ways and his thoughts. So, they mostly humored him. And the boy would lie awake in his bed at night, wondering about his life and why he felt so lost among the villagers. And sometimes, he would cry, and sometimes, he would be angry. But when he heard the call of the wolf on the mountain, right away he knew that here was a voice the likes of which he'd not heard before. Here was a voice that spoke to him of the feelings no one else knew that he had. And lying there and listening with every fiber of his body, he knew he had to seek out this wolf, and know from it, why it cried in the night. Oh, he'd heard the stories of the teeth, the tongue, the eyes so red and burning, but nothing would do except that he had to know that wolf for himself.

———

"Why are people always so afraid? What are they scared of?"

This is my question to the Old Man.

"They're afraid of things they cannot see. They're scared of things they don't understand."

"Yeah, but *why* are they like that?"

"Because the message of fear is everywhere... on TV, in school, and in the church. 'Don't eat this, don't eat that, it will kill you'...'; 'Children, you better pass the test or you'll get left behind at school...', 'Hey, slave worker, you better conform to the soulless routines of your job or you'll be fired...', 'To my congregation, fear God. Don't fail in loving Him the way I've ordered you, because if you don't there's a severe price to pay'."

"I like the boy of this story. He's brave."

"Like you, I imagine," says Old Man.

"I'm not afraid of anything. Mama says people are not born with the spirit of fear."

"Your mama has it right. We're not meant to be fearful. It has no place if you want to survive in this world."

I ask the Old Man if he wants me to keep reading.

"Tomorrow," he tells me. "Same time. It'll be our story hour. Remember, our secret," he says.

The Old Man quietly goes back inside, leaving me all by myself again. But I no longer feel so alone.

SIXTEEN

H annah has a dream.

It is cold—the damp, grating cold of late autumn. Darkness makes a slow approach, as the sun begins to set well past the horizon. Hannah stands in a nearly vacant schoolyard with only a handful of children by her side. Slowly, each child slips away from her care, as they run into their parents' arms. In the short distance, Hannah sees her father standing alone on the other side of a tall, wired fence. He motions for her to come to him.

The metal fence divides the space between them. The father gives Hannah a warm smile. "I am pleased with you. Do you re-member what I told you?"

"Yes, yes, always stay on the Road Less Traveled."

"Never stray off its path."

"Yes, I know."

The father points to a child waiting alone by the school's red doors. The child sits next to the door, reading a book. The father says, "You left one behind."

Hannah walks over to a little girl. She is eight years old. Her skin is the shade of chestnut, and she has raven-colored hair that flows, coarse and untamed. Hannah does not know this child, so she asks, "Where did you come from, princess?"

The little girl looks up from her book, smiles, and says, "I have always been here." Then she nods in the direction of the fence where Hannah once stood. "Your father, what did he say?"

"He was reminding me to stay on the path he told me to."

"Is that all he said?"

"And that he is pleased with me."

The little girl returns to her book, but not before saying, "He is pleased because you don't know the things he knows."

Hannah is startled by the harsh words coming from a mere child. "I only need to know my father, and that which he knows to be right for me."

"He wants you to stay like me... a child. He'll never have to tell you the Truth if you stay like a child. Grown-ups never tell the Truth."

"Why do you say such things, little girl?"

"Because I see the way they lie every day."

"Lies? Even here at school, little girl?"

"Yes, especially here at school. This place is just like any place in the world. It's not a place where they'll ever teach us the Truth. They won't teach us what we need to know to be a true human

being, a strong human being. They pacify us. They teach us easy things that don't really matter. They teach us things that only end up glorifying them."

Hannah looks to where her father once stood. She wants to ask him if he has hidden the Truth. But he is no longer there. So, Hannah turns to the little girl to tell her that she doesn't know that of which she speaks. But the young child has vanished too.

Hannah awakes and dreams no more.

SEVENTEEN

It seems Mama is having a hard time falling asleep. She must be having bad dreams—again. And so, like on those other nights when she can't go to sleep, I hear Mama go outside to sit on our front steps to take in some night air. That leaves me free to do as I please.

I sneak upstairs to her studio. I am searching for that black portfolio. The one Mama was looking at earlier. I see that it's set on a paint-splattered chair next to a bare easel in the corner. It has about twenty pages for artwork. I begin leafing through it. I see nothing. Perhaps this is the wrong book. But I keep going, until I notice that there is indeed work about halfway through. It's not Mama's work, but the work of a little girl. There is no name on the paper, but the little girl has drawn a picture of her family at a park with grass, but neither trees nor sun. Perhaps it's during a picnic. I can't really say. But there are arrows pointed towards each member of her family and labels—Mommy, Brother, Sister, Grandma, and Me.

On the next page, there is a piece of writing. It's titled, "My Quiet Place."

> *My quiet place is in my soul because when I'm mad sometimes, I talk to myself. When I look for a church book I feel very happy because I know that GOD is telling my soul to communicate with me somehow. I know He is watching my every move and listening to every word and thought.*

Beneath the writing is a drawing of a girl who is saying with a smile, "I love myself." Along with the illustration of the girl, is a book with the title *All About My Soul*. Next to this is a drawing of an open book with jagged lines of pretend words and a heart in the middle of the page.

I turn the portfolio page. There is nothing else, except more blank pages. The little girl on these pages is a mystery to me; just like all of the students that Mama teaches. All I know is that this little girl is like all of the kids Mama teaches—she is from a place called Gilead.

Mama teaches in a school that is in the heart of the projects, the Gilead Houses. It's a decaying brick city of small houses clustered around one huge tower of a building. I don't know much about Gilead because Mama doesn't talk about the place. Mama doesn't talk about her students. She never says anything good or anything bad. Not to me during the Quiet Hour, and not to her friends. I guess you can say Mama's silence reveals a lot about how she feels about life there. It's a place so bad that Mama has to hide to away a little girl's work up in her studio.

I close the portfolio and place it back where I found it. There is nothing for me to know about this little girl. She is just another mystery. She's just another lost child of Gilead.

EIGHTEEN

The Old Man is stirred from his sleep.

There is a rustling of footsteps from the floor above, and then the soft and muted creak of the front door as it opens slowly. The Old Man feels a presence outside his window. When he peeks through the blinds, he sees Hannah taking a seat on the front stoop. The Old Man glances over at his clock and sees that it is late, a little less than an hour past midnight. The Old Man goes outside to join her.

Hannah gives him a warm, though weary, smile as he takes a seat by her side. She says to the Old Man, "I know why you've come back. You wanted to see what became of that little girl you used to know."

The Old Man stays quiet. Hannah then asks, "What did you expect to find?"

"I was hoping to see that perfect smile that I always remembered."

"Have you?"

"What I see now is a soft smile, a quiet smile."

"What more were you hoping for?"

"A little joy behind the smile."

Hannah looks away from the Old Man, choosing to stare up at stars splashed across the night sky. "There is joy in my house. There always has been."

The Old Man asks Hannah, "Do you remember how you and I used to talk? You were always so full of questions."

"Questions that always went unanswered."

This makes the Old Man smile. "What would you like to know?"

"You don't have answers to the questions I now have."

"You never know. Try me."

Hannah shifts uneasily. Finally, she says, "I wonder whether or not we can really protect our children from the bad things of this world."

"You shouldn't trouble yourself with questions you know the answer to."

"My father told me that he could. And I have told my own child that I can. But it's not the truth."

"That's because the truth is hard to accept. You can't protect your children from the bad things of this world. It's something you already know."

"So, should we just give up? Not even try."

"You never stop trying. The truth is not set in stone. The truth can change."

"I don't understand. How can the truth change?"

"People's idea of God has changed. God was once seen as vengeful and spiteful. Then a new book comes along, and now God is defined by one word—Love. As man elevates his thinking, he redefines the truth."

"Men redefine the truth in order to justify their own aims and desires."

"Well, maybe we can just hope for a day when men elevate the way they behave towards one another. That will be their aim and desire."

"I can't imagine people ever being concerned with elevating their thinking and elevating the way they act towards one another."

"Well, you will have to believe they will if you ever want the answer to your question to become, 'Yes, I can protect my children from the bad things in this world'."

"That will mean evil no longer exists in the world. It will mean that evil won't win."

"Doesn't sound very likely," says the Old Man, just as much to himself as to Hannah.

For a moment, the words seem to go unacknowledged, until Hannah asks, "The world will never make any sense, will it?"

"It doesn't have to. Little children need an answer for everything. They need everything to make sense to them. But as you get older, you come to learn that it's best not to go around asking so many questions. Maybe it's time for grown-ups to stop acting like children, always asking, 'Why? Why? Why? Why are things the way they are?' Trying to answer the 'whys' of life will only aggravate you. In the end, needing to know 'why,' doesn't matter."

"Sounds like you don't think life has meaning," says Hannah.

"I don't concern myself with assigning meaning. I just try to accept that life is maddening... unexplainable. There's pleasure. There's pain. That's its meaning. Just embrace it. Let it be so. The meaning of life is beyond our understanding. Once we all realize that we don't know much about anything, there'll be less pain and heartache."

NINETEEN

There's a giant tree that stands tall and strong, right in the middle of the park. Its branches are clustered together and stretch out far and wide, letting just the right amount of sunshine burst through its branches and leaves. You can't feel the blazing heat of the sun. The tree is untouched. There are no names carved into its trunk. Nor is there any graffiti. It is perfect.

The park is a quiet and peaceful place. It's a perfect spot to just soothe your mind. I think that's why Mama likes coming here with me. She brings her sketchpad and finds a nice, quiet seat on one of the benches, set just outside the wire fence leading into the park. The park is a place where she is able to just chill and relax. Mama lets me race ahead. She says I can do so because she has to gather her art materials. But I know Mama is just being nice. She doesn't want people to think I'm a mama's boy.

My new friend, Pretty Girl, is by the swing set again. She is the only one in the park. To look at Pretty Girl now, you wouldn't think it's the same person. She is swinging high and she is swinging with no fear. When I ride up to her, she smiles.

She wears the same pink and green outfit from yesterday. Still clean, still pressed, still looking almost brand new, but the same clothes, nonetheless. Pretty Girl still has on the cute engraved anklet with the fine diamonds. I point to it, and ask, "Where did you get that?"

"It found me. It was just lying there in this other playground I used to go to."

"You mean somebody lost it."

"I like to say somebody left it just for me."

I want to tell Pretty Girl that nobody would do something crazy like that, but I don't want to be cruel. Besides, she's soaring so high now. She may not be able to hear me.

Pretty Girl nods in the direction of one of the park benches. I steal a look around the giant tree, and see that Mama has just sat down. She is flipping through her sketchpad.

"Your Mama's beautiful."

Before I can ask Pretty Girl how she knows that's my Mama, she says, "You look like her. The only difference is, she is sad. You should tell your mom that she doesn't have to be. Everything is OK."

Pretty Girl is smart. Someone who, like the Old Man says, seems mindful of things around her. She has Mama pegged right. Mama is a little sad. I want to tell Pretty Girl that Mama hasn't always been like that. It's just been a slight change I've noticed recently—it's a sadness that she'll slip into every now and then. I want to tell Pretty Girl that Mama is usually happy whenever I'm around her. That she always, no matter how sad she may feel inside, tries to smile for me. This is what I want to tell Pretty Girl, but I'm distracted by what I see at the other end of the park. The Thin Man is standing by the park's back gate. He, too, looks the same as before, his face again hidden by his baseball cap. He keeps very still. He doesn't have to motion for Pretty Girl to come.

"Your father is here."

Pretty Girl just smiles at me. Her swing comes to a near stop and she hops off. Thin Man is outside the park on the other side of the fence. He has already started to walk away. I don't take it personally that Pretty Girl just up and leaves. I'm used to it now. I watch Pretty Girl catch up to the Thin Man. They're headed off down a path that leads towards the dingy tower that looms tall and high in the horizon, the Tower of Gilead. But before Pretty Girl disappears out of sight, she looks back my way and waves goodbye to me. I feel better than I did before.

I pop a wheelie all the way to Mama. She's impressed that I can ride up for so long on one wheel. Mama claps softly and gives me that sweet, quiet smile of hers. Perhaps Pretty Girl has it all wrong. Mama doesn't seem so sad.

Mama is working on the same drawing from the day before. She is using the same colored pencils, powder blue and white. I can see that it won't be like Mama's normal work. It won't be abstract. It'll be something more life-like. It's like she's working on a sky with clouds.

"Mama, you're not sad, are you?"

"What makes you ask that?"

"That's what a little girl said."

"What girl?"

"The one that was by the swings. You didn't see her?"

Mama peeks around the giant tree, and says, "No, I didn't."

"She's gone now. But she saw you. She says you're real pretty but seem a little sad."

Mama invites me to come sit with her. She hugs me close.

"I'm never sad when you're around."

"That's what I wanted to tell her."

"Did this little girl say anything else?"

"She said something like, 'There's no need to be sad. Everything is OK.'"

TWENTY

Fox's task is simple: follow the Old Man.

This is what the Merchant has ordered him to do. And the reason is simple enough—someone has dared to cross their path. So the time has now come to learn his story. What Fox, the good soldier, has learned so far is that there's not much of a story to tell—not yet at least. The Old Man lives on a quiet tree-lined street, down in the basement apartment of a tidy brownstone home.

And so, as he had done the day before, Fox has returned to the peaceful street that he had followed the Old Man to. He positions himself in the side alleyway of a four-story high apartment building across the street from the Old Man's home. He stands hidden in the shadows, and he waits.

He is surprised to see the Boy.

Fox remembers him from the pizza shop. And he remembers how there was something about the Boy that he liked.

Though smaller than most kids his age, what Fox saw in the Boy was a feistiness that didn't allow him to become easy prey. A warrior's spirit. The Boy is on his bike, and has stopped in front of the home. He hops off the bike and begins to carry it up the front steps. Fox glances down the street to see if perhaps the Old Man is following behind. Fox doesn't see the Old Man.

He sees the mother instead. She is beautiful. What is her role in the Old Man's story?

Fox steps out of the shadows to get a better look at the mother as she holds open the door for the Boy. She lets her child enter before she follows closely behind and the two disappear inside.

"There's a woman and a boy. They live above the Old Man."

This is what Fox tells the Merchant, who has no noticeable reaction. There is just a slight, knowing grin. The Merchant leans against the cash register set up at the front of the store. He is waiting for Fox to tell him more.

"Anything else?"

"No, I'll check him out again tomorrow."

The Merchant begins counting out the day's money, and without looking up at Fox, he tells him, "There won't be a need for that."

CHAPTER

TWENTY-ONE

"I will trust and not be afraid."
—Isaiah 12:2

In the living room where Mama and I spend the Quiet Hour,
there is a wooden bookcase that reaches almost to the ceiling. The middle rows have a few scattered pictures. Most of
them are of me, mostly from picture days at school. Class
photos and solo shots, from kindergarten to fourth grade.
There is one black-and-white photo of the Candy Man and
the Pretty Lady Dame from their wedding day. And there's
one of Mama and the Candy Man standing in front of his
store. Mama is no more than five years old and she's leaning
up against her father's leg. Her smile is as wide and bright as
it's ever been. But what I hadn't noticed up until now is the
man standing in the background, leaning against the side of
the front door and keeping a watchful eye. It's the Old Man,

only younger. He is clean-shaven and has the same bald head; his goatee has no salt.

I sneak a quick look out the living room window and I see the Old Man. He is standing quietly in the stairwell down to his apartment. He has his switchblade out and is using it to meticulously carve up a mango. The Old Man looks up from his fruit and sees me in the window. He flicks his knife closed and points to his watch. He whispers the words, "It's time." I smile. The Old Man is keeping his word. He's waiting for me to continue my story.

———— ∿ ————

And so one day before the sun rose, the boy set out on the road to the mountain, where it was said the wolf made his den. It was a long road and a steep one, but the boy took no stick and wore no hat to guard him from the sun. It was a dangerous journey, to be sure, but the boy took no weapon to defend himself. And though the country was barren and rocky and not fruitful where he was going, the boy took no food, nor drink to sustain him. And though he'd never been out this way before, he followed no map but went the way of his heart. It was sometime at the end of a day's travel that he began to grow thirsty and the emptiness in his stomach began to make itself known. He walked, becoming even more thirsty, until darkness overtook him, and he was forced to stop for the night in some trees near the road. And as he sat hungry and thirsty in the growing darkness, he thought for a moment, about turning back and rushing back to the village.

But he knew that was not the way for him. So, he sat for a long while shivering in the night and then lay down finally to sleep. In his dreams, the moon shone silver on the frosty stones, the air was clear and crisp, and the voice of the wolf rang out from the top of one of the peaks, calling out the way ahead, perhaps his way. He awoke in the dawn with a start, wondering if the dream had been real, and the wolf had actually called in the night.

"It was easy for the boy to go off on his journey. He doesn't seem to care about the people he's leaving behind."

"Sounds a little selfish, doesn't it?" asks the Old Man.

"Yes, it does."

"He could stay and live the life other people want him to. What do you think about that?"

That's not such an easy question. I think hard on that one. Finally, I say, "I suppose that's not fair to the boy."

The Old Man smiles.

"But his mama will be sad when she realizes he has left."

"She has her own life to live," says the Old Man. "It's time for the boy to live his."

"So, you're saying it's OK to be kind of selfish?"

"When you're in pursuit of something meaningful to you."

"I don't know. It still sounds kind of wrong."

"Well, let me ask you this, what are you taught in your church?"

"To follow the word of God. To live the way God wants you to."

"Think about the things they tell you in school. Stand in line... don't talk... do math lesson at the same hour each day... do you your writing at eleven... science at twelve on Friday."

It sounds funny the way the Old Man puts it. But I tell him, "Yes. I'm taught to follow my teachers. To do as they say, when they say."

"See, you're constantly being told how you should live. Worse, you're constantly being told how you should think."

"It's a little confusing. Sounds like you think people can be selfish, and be cruel and say, 'I'm just following my heart.' That's doesn't sound so right, either."

"Why not?"

"Because I don't live in this world by myself. I can't just do whatever I want without thinking about other people. I mean, places like my church and my school want what's best for me."

"I'm not so sure of that."

"I am. Because they're giving us rules and thoughts set up for people to live and act the right way with one another. That's not a bad thing."

The Old Man smiles at me again. "No, it's not a bad thing if you're brought up to believe that there ought to be rules. But rules are about control."

I tell the Old Man I don't see how people can live any other way. "The world would go crazy."

"The world has gone crazy *with* rules. How worse off can the world be, if we all just went about doing our own thing? Survival of the fittest."

"What does that mean?"

"It means only the strongest survive." The Old Man points to his head and says, "And most of that strength that's required for you to survive is up here... in your mind."

"I don't think Mama and I would stand a chance in a world without rules and order."

"Don't sell the world short. People can love and support one another without being told they have to. Without being told how to do so. It's already inherent in you. Some say, 'It's the God in you.' It's something already inherent in everybody."

"So, I shouldn't listen to Mama, my teachers, my pastor? I shouldn't listen to you, either, huh?"

The Old Man smiles at me. "Is that really what you think I'm telling you?"

I tell the Old Man, no, that's not what I think he means.

"Wise people—whether a teacher, a pastor, a mailman—they will share themselves in a way that will get you to open up your mind and be free to explore and embrace new ideas."

"So, I guess I should always listen?"

"Yes, always be quiet and still, so that you can listen and then do what?" asks the Old Man.

"Learn," I say.

"Yes, so that in the end, you won't just blindly accept what people tell you. And when you keep still, listen and learn, then you'll be able to do what?"

"Think for myself."

I close the book and set it down beside me. Nothing is said right away. But then I tell the Old Man, "Outside of Mama, I never really been around someone who cared enough to ask what I think about things. I wonder if my granddad was still alive if this is the way he would speak to me. If he would care enough about how I see things. About what I think. Like you do."

"He would."

"It's hard for me to ask Mama about him. I can tell she doesn't like talking about granddad. She has this lost look whenever his name is mentioned. I don't know what it is that he could have done to make her feel so ashamed. Mama says he was a good man, but maybe she isn't telling the truth. Maybe he did something so evil that she's ashamed."

"Your mama told you the truth about your grandfather. He was a good man. Don't ever let anybody make you see different."

There's movement behind us. The Old Man and I turn and find Mama standing quietly in the doorway. I don't know how long she's been there. I don't know if she has heard what the Old Man and I have been speaking about. But she seems at ease and she smiles at us. She tells me that it's getting late, and that it's time to come inside. Though the sun has disappeared somewhere far off in the distance, there is a faint glow that remains. I could perhaps ask Mama to stay outside a little longer. But Mama seems happy and at peace. This is not a battle I need to win. I do as I'm told. I listen to Mama.

TWENTY-TWO

Hannah has watched the Boy and the Old Man from afar. She has listened to the quiet murmur of their conversations, and she has heard the hushed tones in which they speak to one another. It's like a language that is all their own. Hannah tells herself that there is no need to worry or feel threatened by the Old Man's presence in the Boy's life. The Old Man brings yet another set of eyes and another voice to help the Boy see and understand the world.

Hannah knows that the Old Man's routine is to return outside for a late evening cigarette a few hours after the Boy has been put to bed. So, Hannah steps outside and sees the Old Man standing in the corner of his doorway with a cigarette in his hand.

"Good evening," says the Old Man.

"The Boy is asleep," says Hannah. "Thought I'd come out and join you."

No words are spoken at first. Hannah glances over at the Old Man. She realizes there is much that she doesn't know about him. Perhaps he has shared a bit of himself with her son. Hannah asks the Old Man, "What do you and my son talk about so quietly amongst yourselves?"

The Old Man smiles and says, "We talk about stories and the meanings we see in them. You can learn a lot about a person from what they take away from a story."

"And what have you learned about my son?"

"That he's very smart. He's a thinker. He's not afraid to ask questions."

Hannah smiles, but is at a loss for words—but only for a moment. "I imagine he often asks about my father."

"He wants to know his history."

"Because to know your history," says Hannah, "is to know your destiny."

"That's what they say. But the Boy may not need know his personal history. He'll create his own destiny. He'll create his own path."

"He has no choice but to do so."

"And that's OK," the Old Man tells Hannah. "Sometimes, your history can be a burden. Sometimes, your history is used against you and becomes something that holds you back and keeps you in your place."

Hannah knows the Old Man has questions of his own. "I'm sure there is more you want to ask me."

"Tell me, what does the Boy know?"

"You mean does he know what happened between me and his father?"

"Yes."

Hannah struggles for the right words, so she says nothing at first.

"There's no need for him to know, especially since his father just took off and seemingly vanished into thin air."

"And the Boy never asks what type of man he was or why he's gone?"

"No. The Boy has learned to live with 'I don't know' as an answer. So have I."

The Old Man reaches over and touches Hannah on her chin and tilts her head gently to the side. He sees the faded scar by her jaw. And as he remembers, the left eye with the soft, pretty lashes continues to flutter out of rhythm ever so subtly.

Hannah manages a quiet smile, and says, "The Boy doesn't need to know everything. All he needs to know is that here, in this house, with me, he is loved."

"Yes, that is enough," says the Old Man.

He walks over to the front gate and closes it behind him. Hannah asks where he is going so late at night.

"Just for a little walk around the old neighborhood. Something I've been doing each night since I've been back."

Hannah tells the Old Man, "Be safe, out there."

It is late. That time, just around midnight, when the darkness of the night is deep and unsettling. Yet the Old Man walks with ease. He steps confidently past the darkened doorways and alleys along the main thoroughfare. All is relatively silent.

"Still, you know not the truth?"

The voice behind the broken English is calm and familiar. The Old Man doesn't flinch at seeing a man standing in the open doorway of The Golden Sun. He is around the same age as the Old Man. He is a short and slightly built. The clothes that he wears do not fit him well; his grease-stained white apron is so big and long that it practically drags on the floor. The paper-made chef's hat that sits askew atop his head is two sizes too big. But he leans confidently against the door of his restaurant. The Chef stops tugging at his wispy mustache, steps aside, and makes a path for the Old Man to enter The Golden Sun.

The Old Man eyes the counter in the back of the restaurant, and sees that the Chef's son is cleaning up for the night. The son is the spitting image of his father, but built stronger and leaner, with hair long enough to be pulled back into a ponytail. The son has the same cautious eyes as the father, and he stares back at the Old Man. The son wonders if the Old Man is on a fool's errand. Nevertheless, he gives the Old Man a knowing nod of respect.

"We closed almost," says the Chef's son. "You want your usual?"

"Yes," says the Old Man.

There are two empty, red tables and four bench seats bolted down to the floor. A massive picture of the Forbidden City hangs on the wall above them. The Old Man takes a seat at the table closest to the door and joins the Chef in looking out onto the street. From the Golden Sun's spot on the corner of the block, the Old Man sees what the Chef sees: a lonely street where nearly every business is closed. All the gates are drawn down on the shops and businesses along the block. The lone exception is the fading light coming from the car service hut, where a cab driver leans against his taxi, smoking a cigarette.

And from the Golden Sun, the Old Man sees the candy shop on the corner at the opposite end of the street.

"Anything?" asks the Old Man.

"I see what you see," says the Chef.

The old candy shop is closed for business. But the gate is only halfway down. Muted light seeps through the slender grills on the gate.

"I don't know what goes on. Could be counting money."

"After an honest day's work?"

The Chef smiles. "Perhaps."

The Chef's son brings over a plate covered with dumplings and slides it in front of the Old Man. He, too, takes a look out the window. The son knows what the Old Man and his father are looking at. Staring at the old candy shop late at night has become a nightly routine.

"Nothing happens there."

"He don't understand," says the Chef to the Old Man.

"Help me, then," says the son.

"Things happened long before your father sent for you," says the Old Man. "It doesn't matter if nothing happens there. All I care about is who comes in and out."

"Who are you looking for?"

The Old Man and the Chef just look at one another. They say nothing. The Chef tells his son to finish cleaning up in the back. "It's time to go home."

"You looking for ghosts," says the son, with a shrug, as he leaves to do as he's told.

The Chef looks over to his friend, the Old Man. "My son has point. You are looking for a ghost. That boy's never coming back. The story goes, Pretty Lady Dame saw to that."

"What else have you heard of the story?"

"Boy harm girl. Candy Man and Pretty Lady Dame avenge their child. Boy vanishes. Simple story."

The Old Man finishes his late-night snack and heads for the door. The Chef unlocks the door and lets him out, but not before asking, "See you tomorrow?"

"Yes," says the Old Man. "Because I believe in ghosts."

TWENTY-THREE

I'm stretched out across the foot of Mama's bed. I'm watching her and trying my best to be patient, so we can make our way to the park again. There's a large mirror atop her dresser that Mama stares into. She's not doing anything but gazing at herself. There's no expression on her face. I wonder what Mama sees. I wonder if Mama sees someone weary of daily trips to the playground.

I tell Mama, "We can do something else if you want."

Mama turns away from the mirror, and looks my way with a smile that's genuine.

"I like going to the park with you."

"You're just saying that."

"No, I'm serious. I do like to go. I want to see if I can prove myself wrong."

"I don't understand. Prove yourself wrong about what?"

"I've come to learn a hard, uncomfortable truth: there are a lot of unloved children in the world. It breaks my heart because unloved children have a way of harming others. I wish it wasn't so. But that's what happens when you have unloved children. They're just out there in the world on their own. They're out there raising themselves because the adults in their lives are too busy to show them love or don't want to show them love or guidance. These unloved children lash out and hurt others. So, I go to that park everyday with you, hoping I will see a whole playground filled with children who are loved."

I wonder if Pretty Girl is one of the unloved children Mama talks of.

I ride up to the park and see Pretty Girl by the swings again. But I stop at the edge of the playground, and I stay hidden out of sight. I don't ride over to her because she is not alone. The Thin Man is there. His face is concealed underneath the same baseball cap he wore both days. I can't see if he's happy or if he's bored. He's just standing on the other side of the fence quietly watching Pretty Girl swing high and free up into the sky.

The Thin Man motions for Pretty Girl to stop. Without saying a word, he turns and starts to walk away. He doesn't wait for her. Pretty Girl rushes off the swing and races after him. She catches up to him and takes his hand. They walk out the opposite end of the park.

I go over to the swing that Pretty Girl was on. It is still swaying back and forth. I take a seat and then notice something sparkling on the ground. It's the anklet that Pretty Girl wears. It somehow fell off without her noticing. I reach for it quickly. But when I glance up, Pretty Girl seems to have disappeared. Before I can put the anklet away, a voice creeps up from behind me.

"What you got there?"

It's Tum Tum. He has appeared from out of nowhere, as usual. But he doesn't enter the playground. He stays on the other side of the fence.

"What is it? Let me see. Bring it here."

At first, I hesitate to go over to him. But I do. I hold it up to Tum Tum. I'm thinking he'll probably think it's nothing special. But the anklet and its diamonds sparkle in the palm of my hand. Tum Tum is amazed by it. Then Tum Tum asks, "What does it say?"

The anklet has a small gold plate with an inscription. I show it to him.

He's astonished and starts to reach for it through the fence. I pull it away from his reach. Tum Tum asks, "You think it costs a lot of money?"

"I'm sure it does. But I don't care about that."

"You should. That's good money you got there. What are you going do with it?"

I shrug. I haven't given it that much thought.

"You should sell it. Those are diamonds. Real ones. They're worth something."

"I won't sell it. I know the girl it belongs to. I just have to find her."

"What girl? Tell me about her."

There's really not much to tell. I've only seen Pretty Girl twice. I tell Tum Tum that wherever Pretty Girl is, the Thin Man is nearby.

"You're talking about ghosts."

"And you're talking crazy."

"Nobody has seen them but you. I come by this park all the time, and I've never seen this little girl and her father. That makes them ghosts."

"Ghosts? You're a fool, Tum Tum."

Tum Tum points towards the Tower of Gilead. Then Tum Tum leans closer to the fence as though he doesn't want anyone else to hear him. "Listen up. I come from Gilead. So, you can choose to not believe me if you want. You won't be the first one to fall for the greatest lie ever."

"And what lie is that?"

"That monsters don't exist. But the stories out of Gilead are true—like the story about a little girl whose stepfather, the devil, took her away. Nobody knows what's become of her. Some wonder if she's even still alive. Most believe that the father has this little girl locked up in a cage and lets her out only in times of darkness. It's said in Gilead that whenever you hear a child cry, it's a warning. Round up your children and protect them because the Devil is coming."

"Sounds like a stupid story to me."

Tum Tum laughs at his own story. "Think what you want. This story is the truth." He straightens up and sits back on his ratty bike that he dropped to the ground by the fence.

"It's boring in this baby park." Tum Tum nods in the direction of Mama who is just getting to the park. "I would ask you to come hang, but I know that your mom won't let you go. See you later, mama's boy."

Tum Tum rides away towards his home in Gilead—laughing at me.

———⌣———

From the park, I can see the Tower of Gilead in the distance. The tip of its grimy brown tower reaches high into the sky. Tum Tum is right; I don't know much about Gilead. What I do know about the place comes from the overflow of kids they've dumped into my school—kids like Tum Tum. He's a Child of Gilead. But how can I take what he says seriously? He's a kid who tries to scare you with stories of a monster-like brother named Scarface, who hides in the shadows. He tells tales of an evil stepdad stealing away children. And Tum Tum likes to spin tales about young gangstas jumping you and runnin' pockets. Tum Tum gets a kick out of talking about people doing the nasty in the stairwell. He tries to spook you with tales of walls filled with posters of missing children. Tum Tum is always talking about how, if you don't know somebody in Gilead, you'll be entering at your own risk. Tum Tum likes spreading fear. I don't believe what he tells me about Gilead.

They're just stories to me. But then again, I did tell you what Mama once said about stories. "Stories don't have to be real. Stories just need to reveal the truth."

When I race over to Mama's quiet spot in the park, I find that she hasn't even taken out her sketchpad. She's just sitting there with her eyes closed, kind of like she's meditating. When she opens her eyes, I'm standing right there.

"Mama, what can you tell me about Gilead?"

"It's a place where people live."

"I know that, Mama. But what do you know about the people? A lot of kids from your school live there."

Mama doesn't say anything. Mama glances off in the direction of the Tower of Gilead. She is quiet, except for a sudden, exhausted sigh that seems prompted by a sadness flowing through her thoughts. Perhaps she is thinking about the little girl of the portfolio? Perhaps some other child of Gilead? I want to ask, but what follows is that look. It's that same dead, lifeless stare that usually falls across her face whenever there's talk of the Candy Man. It's that mask of disillusionment I was telling you about before. But Mama finally speaks up. She doesn't give me an answer. Mama says simply and quietly, "Go and play."

TWENTY-FOUR

The Pastor travels along a path, one he has taken many times before. At a familiar point along the way, the young pastor's pace begins to slow, and his lengthy strides shorten. Up ahead is a home, neat and tidy. Sometimes, a little boy sits out front alone with a book. Sometimes, his mother, who's an artist and a teacher, is out there too with a sketchpad in her lap. The Pastor likes the boy's mannerly ways, while the beauty of the mother awes him. Warm and gentle smiles from mother and child always greet him. The Pastor likes to pause here on his journey. Joy can be found here. There is peace.

But now a stranger sits in their place.

He is a grizzled older man who looks at the young man with a knowing gaze. The stranger seems to understand why the Pastor has stopped by this place.

"The mother and the boy are not here."

The Pastor says, "Thank you." He is about to continue along his way, when the old man says, "The boy told me about you. He says you're a friend."

"I am. And who are you to them?" the young pastor asks.

"I'm a friend as well."

The stranger continues to study the young man, "The boy says you're from their church. He says you're their pastor. That must mean you're in the business of saving lost souls."

"Yes, that is what I do."

"Some would say that makes you a magician."

The young pastor smiles and tells the stranger that there's no magic in what he does.

"Then how do you go about this job of saving souls?"

"You listen to people's stories."

The old man neither smiles nor frowns—he simply nods in understanding. "Well, I should let you go on your way to do God's work. You'll find the mother and boy are up ahead."

The Pastor continues on his way. The stranger is right—the mother and boy can be found along this path. They're alone in the park, just the two of them. The young man slows his steps and watches the boy ride away from his mother.

It occurs to the young pastor just how little he knows about the mother. He knows this pretty lady only through the few words they've shared during the let-out at the end of church service, and the chats when he's paused out in front of her home. Theirs is a relationship of brief, pleasant encounters. It has never been anything beyond that.

The Pastor walks up to her, and says, "Good afternoon."

The pretty lady offers a pleasant smile, and asks, "How are you, Pastor?"

"Fine," the young man says. "It's been a little while since I've seen you. I used to see you at the end of service, even if only for a few minutes. How were the children this year?"

The pretty lady smiles at the young pastor's kinder, more profound way of asking, "How was school this year?"

"Long... and trying."

"You no longer enjoy what you do?"

"It will always bring joy. All day, children surround me. They go out of their way to see me smile. The children say, 'I love you,' a hundred times a day to me. No one can ever take away the beauty that comes with that."

"But I imagine it's hard to keep that smile at times."

"Yes."

"I guess the question is: 'did you learn anything from the children this year?' Teaching goes both ways."

"I've come to learn what my job as a teacher is."

"Which is?" the young pastor asks.

"I'm just a guardian of fragile children who come to us broken. My job isn't so much to teach, but rather to be like a cobbler and put them back together. But I'm not a cobbler. So, I end up just trying to do my best, and show them another path, give them structure. My job is to build up their self-esteem...

show them love. Still, after all that, the end of the school day arrives, and I have to send them back out into the world."

"And the world corrupts."

"The world does more than that. It swallows them whole and takes them away, never to return. And then the world laughs at me, and reminds me how powerless I am to truly help them... to protect them. The world lets me know the futility of noble intentions."

"You must feel hope at some point?"

"My favorite part of the day is when I read stories to the children. Fairy tales and folktales from around the world. They speak of things we all can relate to—courage, family bonds, love. But at the end of the day, they're just stories of monsters and big, bad wolves, and witches and mean giants—things the children don't have to be afraid of because they are not real. I need to teach the children something more important: it's man they should fear. They need to fear man's cruelty. Fear man's ignorance, because man's ignorance makes him dangerous. Man is the real monster."

"You know our doors are always open for you to talk about how you feel."

The pretty lady says softly, "I doubt you have the words to explain away broken children. I doubt you have words that justify why these children are being allowed to suffer."

"Not being able to see or imagine a reason why God might allow something to happen doesn't mean there isn't one. The lack of a clear answer doesn't mean that a credible, but hidden, explanation for such brokenness doesn't exist."

"I have little use for the argument that God has reasons for His actions that go beyond our rational understanding. Nor am I in the mood to hear that suffering is a part of life."

"You have a sense of fair play and justice. Most people do. You have the noble view that people should not suffer… that people should not be excluded, should not die of hunger or be oppressed. But you must acknowledge that this life requires death, destruction, and violence by the strong against the weak. It's natural. So, if this is the reality, how can the non-believer judge the natural world to be wrong, unfair, and unjust?"

"It's hard to blindly accept the notion: 'be not afraid, at the end of the day victory is assured if you just believe.' That is just a notion religion sells to people in order to pacify us like little children. They're just things said to us in order to explain away the bad things that happen."

The young pastor has learned that when people are in pain, sometimes the best thing to do is offer them a respectful silence. He says nothing. He just watches her. The young pastor waits for the pretty lady to say more.

"I shouldn't talk this way around you," she says, in a near whisper. "I shouldn't talk with so much doubt. I shouldn't sound like I'm questioning God. Not to you."

"God is big enough for your questions. These questions can, one day, end up reaffirming your faith."

With a smile meant to disarm, the pretty lady asks, "Is that truly so?"

The young pastor tells her, "It is what I believe. You know, we all strive to live as if it's better to live in peace rather than in war; that it's better to tell the truth instead of lie; to care and nurture, rather than destroy. These choices are not pointless. It matters which way we choose to live. The struggle is, if you believe the universe is empty and one where there is no higher authority, then who is to say one choice is better than the other? Who is to say whether or not we should be loving or cruel? If that's the case, in the end, it will make no difference."

"What does it mean to believe then?"

"There are two options: we can believe in this empty universe with no God but still choose to live life as though our choices have meaning, that we know the difference between love and cruelty. But that's having one's cake and eating it too. You get the benefit of having a God without the cost of following Him. But there's a second way, and the one I choose: live as though you *know* for sure there is a God. Choose to live as though beauty and love have meaning; choose that there is meaning in life; chose that humans have inherent dignity. You accept all this because you *know* God exists. Because, in the end, it is dishonest to live as though God exists but not as though He was the one who has given you all the gifts."

TWENTY-FIVE

There's a stranger along the Road Less Traveled. It is Fox, the young guy I first saw at Injun Rah's. He is standing by one of the park benches. He is on the outside of the playground, in the area where the older boys used to hang out and play basketball. However, the two hoops now hang broken on the fence. No one can use them anymore. But Fox is here now. And like at the pizza shop, he is watching me. Mama warned me about talking to strangers. But I don't always listen. Since Mama sent me on my way, I ride over to Fox. Maybe he'll talk to me.

Fox greets me simply from his side of the fence. "What's up, little man?"

"I'm good." Then I ask, "What are you doing here? I've never seen you out this way before."

"That's because you didn't know me before."

"Where do you live?" I ask.

Fox points in the direction of the dingy tower off in the distance.

"So, you're from Gilead, too?"

"Who do you know from over there?"

"Everybody. I know Tum Tum, and Pretty Girl, and a few other kids from my school. And now I know you."

"That's not everybody."

"My mama works over there, too."

"She's a teacher."

I can't tell if he says this as a fact or question. It's kind of creepy that he would say it at all. So, I ask him "You know her?"

Fox looks over in the direction of Mama. It looks like she's talking to Pastor from our church. Fox points to her, "That's her over there, isn't it?"

"Perhaps it is. Perhaps not."

Fox smiles for the first time. He seems pleased. "You have some smarts. I guess you know it's bad enough that you're talking to strangers."

"You're not really a stranger to me."

"I doubt that's what your mother would think if she saw me talking to you."

"It doesn't matter what she thinks. What matters is what I think. What matters is what I know."

"And what is it that a little boy like you knows?"

"I know you are in no hurry to get home if you're hanging out in this deserted park talking to me. Is there nothing waiting for you in Gilead?"

"Nothing, and no one."

"That can't be right."

"Only a kid thinks that everything must be 'right'."

"Well, that's what I am... a kid... remember."

Fox laughs and says, "True. Just don't end up grown and still thinking and acting like a child."

I look over to where Mama is sitting. She is now alone. Pastor has left her. And now she is looking around the park with concern in her eyes. She is searching for me. But Mama doesn't see me just yet. I know it's best I get back to her before she finds me. I tell Fox that I have to go.

As I start to ride away, Fox calls to me, and says, "There's a reason why I came this way. Just wanted to pass on some advice. A warning."

Fox is sounding scary. "A warning?"

"Yeah. Be careful, little man. Be mindful of everybody and everything around you." Fox then looks over in the direction of Mama. "Go, she needs you."

TWENTY-SIX

The Old Man sits alone on the front steps of Hannah's home. He tells himself, *be patient*. The time has not arrived for him to go back home yet. But the Old Man knows he could do so now while Hannah and child are away. He could do so without so much as a goodbye. The Old Man knows he could slip back into the shadows from whence he came. He could go back home where life is simple. He could go before someone here can remind him of who he is.

"What's up, Killer?"

The Old Man looks up and sees the Merchant standing by the front gate. The Old Man had not seen or even heard him approach. But there the Merchant stands. The sight of this stranger doesn't startle the Old Man. The Old Man calmly asks, "Do you know me?"

"Nah, I don't know you," says the Merchant. He pulls out a Black & Mild. He lights up the white-tipped cigar. "But I know what you are."

"You speak in riddles," says the Old Man. "Tell me, what is it that I am."

"I believe I just did... Killer."

"You don't know me."

"You can tell yourself that if you like. But perhaps I'm not here to share with you those things that I know to be true about you."

"Then why come at all?"

"To share this knowledge with those who don't."

"I don't know what you're getting at."

"No, Killer, I think you do."

The Merchant takes a long, hard look down the street. The Boy is approaching on his bike. Hannah has yet to turn the corner. "The Boy doesn't know what you are. And I doubt the mother, Hannah, knows either. That's who I'm really here for. They ought to know the truth. Unless we can come to an agreement that the silence of that truth has a price."

"More riddles."

"Riddles. Truth. You will acknowledge to me what you are. And you, and perhaps Hannah, will pay me well for that truth."

The Merchant turns and walks away, leaving the Old Man to wonder just what price must be paid to keep the truth hidden from Hannah and child.

TWENTY-SEVEN

The Boy rose, still hungry, and continued on his way. Soon the path grew steeper and rockier. As the sun was moving high and the day was warming, the boy noticed a flock of birds swooping and playing in a small pool beside the road.

The boy rushed to the water, fell on his belly and drank his fill. When he rose, the birds were watching him silently from a nearby tree limb. Realizing he had interrupted their play, he smiled and thanked them for letting him drink and continued on the path. Though his thirst was slaked, the emptiness was still burning deep in his belly. And as he walked, once again thoughts came to him of quitting; of just sitting down under a tree to wait for whatever might happen to happen. And what if he never got up again? Would anyone miss him or come to find him? But something told him, this was not the end of his journey. If he did not continue, he would never know what was at the end of the path or why the wolf cried in the night. And so, he decided to continue walking, knowing not what lay ahead of him.

———⌣———

The Old Man is distracted. So, I stop reading *Wolf and Boy*. I ask the Old Man, "Should I continue?"

"You can stop there," he says.

I close the book and start to head inside. But the Old Man stops me, and asks, "What has your mama told you about me?"

"Nothing really," I say. "She's letting me get to know you on my own."

"And what have you come to know about me?"

"You're pretty serious. I guess that comes with being a soldier. But everyone loves a soldier. That should always make you happy."

Old Man smiles, and says, "It all depends on what war you're fighting. If people don't approve of the war, they tend to judge you harshly. They'll call you killer."

"I'm not sure I understand."

"In time, you will."

TWENTY-EIGHT

". . . Never tire of doing what is right."
—2 Thessalonians 3:13

Upstairs in her studio, Hannah has a large cardboard box where she keeps every note handed to her by a child, and every modest, heart-felt drawing done on loose-leaf paper. The box also contains special writings that have been left behind in dog-eared marble notebooks. The writings and drawings remind her that these children will always have a voice. These students will always be of worth. These children have not been lost.

They remind Hannah, too, that she teaches in an unforgiving world, in which children come and go. Sometimes, they leave without warning. Sometimes, they leave without ever saying goodbye. Some are children of shelters whose families pick up and flee at a moment's notice in search of a home. Some are foster children moving from family to family. And then some are children who simply disappear and vanish.

"Beware of the wolf in sheep's clothing."

Hannah knows that there are words, often cited but rarely heeded. There are words that hold the key to keeping the children out of harm's way. "Beware of the wolf in sheep's clothing." Hannah often wonders, *why did I not accept this as truth?*

———

Princess was a quiet girl, smaller than most of the other children her age. Hannah loved the child's pleasant ways. Princess was a bright student with an artist's spirit. If Hannah is honest with herself, she'll admit that Princess was her favorite.

And one afternoon, Princess was stolen away.

Hannah remembers having seen Princess with the man before. She had seen him along with the Mother. He had been introduced to Hannah as the Father. But the Father always stayed a few steps behind. He was always slightly out of the picture. The Father would lurk in the background and look at Hannah with a disarming smile. On many occasions when school was over, Hannah would see the Father, and the Mother, and they would take Princess and walk out of the schoolyard together— like a family.

Hannah remembers that there was nothing scary about the Father. He was tall and slender, and wore loosely fitted clothes. Hannah never looked directly into his eyes because he always donned tinted eyeglasses or shades.

On this day he came alone. And Princess ran into his arms, which were opened wide. And together, Princess and the Father began to walk out of the schoolyard. Then with a simple glance back, followed by a wave, Princess disappeared holding his hand.

The Mother came shortly thereafter, and asked, "Have you seen Princess?"

Hannah remembers looking back at the Mother with a quizzical look. "Don't you know? Princess left with..." Hannah remembers not knowing what to say next. She remembers how foolish it would sound for her to continue on and say, "... with a stranger." For that was what the father was to her—a stranger.

Later, under the scrutiny of a Detective's disapproving glare, Hannah was asked a flurry of questions.

"What was he wearing?"

"I don't remember."

"The little girl, did she seem afraid?"

"She ran into his arms."

"Did he say why he came for the girl?"

"No... no... he just appeared."

"Did he say where he was taking her?"

"No."

"Is it common for you to hand over a child to anyone who comes for them?"

"No... no... I thought I knew him. He is her father."

Hannah soon tuned out the questions. She answered with long blank stares, subtle nods of and shakes of her head, and outright silence.

They have no right to judge me because monsters exist in this world.

Hannah keeps Princess' artwork away from the other children's work. She has it hidden deep inside the middle pages of a black portfolio that she keeps buried away behind a stack of easels in her studio. She tells herself, *this work does not belong to me.* Every night she takes time to read about Princess' Quiet Place. Hannah takes a long look at her drawing of a family. And she cries.

TWENTY-NINE

It's easy to fall into a routine in summer: wake up, go to the park, come home, have dinner, go to bed. Wake up; go to the park, and so on, and so on. Routines aren't bad. The sun rises every morning in the East and sets in the West. The Earth spins on its axis in the same manner every day. "Routines remind everyone that there's order in the world." That's what Mama says.

But she'll also tell you, too, that if you're not careful, they can lead to a life of no imagination. In my little world of school and church, it's all about routine; doing and saying the same things, all the time. In school, it's the morning lineup, word study, reading period, writing workshop, math, and a little science and social studies thrown in every now and then. And the class right next door to me, they're required to follow the exact same routine as us. I imagine that's why so many teachers are grumpy, it's like they're going to work at a boring, old factory every day.

And each Sunday, at church, I witness another routine. Service starts with praise and worship, followed by prayer, then a skit by the drama ministry, then offering time, then finally, the sermon. There's even a routine in the Word. At some point near the end of Pastor's sermon each and every Sunday, he is going to talk about giving thanks to God for waking you up this morning; for that job He got you; for how He helped you with your rent; for how He helped you when you didn't have a job or the rent. School and church should be the last places on Earth where you have the same old, same old. Mama says, "Anything dealing with knowledge and getting one's mind right, and anything having to do with the spirit and the soul, shouldn't be concerned about routine and the clock."

So, Mama is getting us away from the summer routine. Mama's says we're going to take our Quiet Hour away from home, and go take it in peace and quiet down by The River. Usually anything related to the Quiet Hour is just Mama and me. But Mama is not sticking to the routine—she is inviting the Old Man to come with us. Maybe she also sees that the Old Man is distracted.

⌣

I don't think the Old Man is used to being asked for his company. It is taking him forever just to change and get dressed. But eventually he finishes, and he comes out looking crisp. He has on this lime-green silk shirt, his jeans, and a pair of brown loafers. If I didn't know better, I'd say he is headed out on a date.

Where we are going is beyond the Road Less Traveled. We're going down to the River. It's a short bus ride and an even shorter walk through quiet, tree-lined streets in a quiet part of the City called the Heights. The streets are narrow and though the homes are brownstones like ours, they're grander with large bay windows that allow you to peek inside and see fancy chandeliers that hang from ceilings so high they seem to reach to the sky.

Mama and the Old Man don't say much on our way to the River. And neither do I. Mama has taught me that it's not my place to speak and bring attention to myself when I'm around adults. Keep a respectful silence. That's what Mama has taught me. So, I just listen to Mama and the Old Man talk. The Old Man does most of the talking. And I begin to learn more about him as he does. I hear him talk about the City, a city he says, "I really know so little about." I listen and I hear him talk of rarely stepping beyond that part of the Madness where the Candy Man's shop was.

We arrive at the promenade. There is a bench, one of many that line its bank. We take a seat and look out onto the River. Mama tells the Old Man how she likes to come out this way when the weather is nice. The waters of the River are calm most days. I'm feeling a little tired and I place my head on Mama's lap. I curl up and fold my legs under me on the bench. I watch the Old Man gaze out at the skyline of the main city that's across the water.

I hear him say, "God gave men the vision to create monuments that reach up to the heavens." The Old Man stops for a moment. When he continues, it's almost as though he's talking to himself. "Where I come from, men don't have such dreams."

Mama wants to know more about the Old Man. She wants to know about this place where men don't have such vision. I'm slowly drifting into sleep. But I hear Mama ask the Old Man, "Tell me your story."

THIRTY

The Old Man has a story to tell.

But the Old Man says, "I don't tell my story to everyone. I only tell those who are believers. You must believe in miracles."

⁓

There once was a Young Girl. She was a runaway. Her father had abandoned the family. No one knew what happened to him or what became of him. But he left this Young Girl alone with a mother disinterested in loving and caring for her in a meaningful way. So, at the age of fifteen, the Young Girl ran away. She roamed the backcountry roads of the South. Her life was just about finding food and shelter. To do so, she sought out extended family and the kindness of strangers. She'd sleep in their barns, or an extra room, if it was available. This went on for some time.

The Young Girl eventually journeyed to the next town over from where she was born. She wandered upon a little country diner and the small home settled in the backfield behind it. The young girl didn't ask for food and a place to rest right away. She spent a day just watching the place from afar. She came to see that the diner belonged to an older couple. She saw that they were some twenty years or so older than she was. They were childless.

Spider is what everybody called the man. He was long and wiry, with arms and legs that went on for days. And he had a pockmarked face, always covered by the stubble of a two-day old beard. The runaway girl approached Spider long after the wife had gone off to the home out back. She had seen how the couple worked so hard running the business by themselves. Surely, they needed help. Spider was tying up the trash when the Young Girl came up to him. He wasn't surprised to see her. It was almost as though he was expecting her. His first words to her were, "Do you know me?"

The runaway told him, "No."

"Then why are you here, young girl?"

"You and your wife need me. I've seen how you both work so hard. You won't have to pay me. All I need is food and a place to rest my head."

It must have been the Young Girl's boldness. Maybe it was her pretty smile, or her light brown eyes. But Spider took her in. He didn't ask the wife what she thought. He simply told her, "This pretty girl is here to help you. See that she has enough work to do."

People called her 'Miss Radiance', because as a little baby lying in her cradle, she had the brightest, most beautiful smile one could ever see in a child. Miss Radiance grew to be a dutiful wife, who did what she was told by her husband, because she had resigned herself to a life mainly meant to support Spider's ambition to work for no man but himself. Miss Radiance told the Young Girl when to clean and what to clean. She told her who to serve and when. Miss Radiance kept her busy. For the first few months, Miss Radiance didn't speak a word to the Young Girl other than to give her an order. The Young Girl was nothing more than a servant to Miss Radiance.

But in time, the Young Girl became a friend to Miss Radiance. Their relationship grew. During quiet hours when the diner was closed, the girl would sit down on the floor and Miss Radiance, sitting in a chair above her, would comb and braid her hair. And it was here that they would talk. Miss Radiance would often ask, "What are your dreams, Young Girl?"

"I don't have dreams. Not anymore. I always wanted a home. But to dream is silly."

"Do you dream of nice things, like having a family of your own one day?"

"You can't dream of things you know nothing about. I don't know what family is."

"Spider and I dreamed of a family. But some dreams are just not meant to be."

Spider would watch the young girl and Miss Radiance. Spider saw how they would sit on the front porch of the diner and talk when no customers were around, and he saw how they laughed when working together at the close of each day. Spider grew envious and wanted a special relationship with the girl too. But the girl always kept a respectful distance from him. Her eyes rarely met his. So, one night after Miss Radiance had finished with her work and left the diner, Spider returned there. And in the quiet and still-ness of night, Spider cornered the Young Girl, and pulled a neatly wrapped gift from behind his back and handed it to her. "A pretty little girl like you deserves nice things."

The Young Girl was reluctant to open it because she never saw him show such kindness to his wife. But he insisted, "Open it. It's OK." Inside, the girl found an anklet. Spider leaned over and gave the girl a kiss on the forehead. "Here, let me help you put it on."

And Spider got close, very close, and helped the Young Girl with the anklet, and said, "I see how you and Miss Radiance talk. What is it that you talk about?"

The girl believed Spider was a kind man at heart—for he did take her in, after all—so she told him the truth. "We talk about dreams. We talk about believing in them. We talk about dreams that don't come true."

"My wife shouldn't talk about such things." And he was sad-dened and angry because he knew what his wife's dreams were—what his dreams were. Spider walked away from the Young Girl without saying anything more. She watched him disappear into the night, and later, she heard arguing at the home out in back of the diner. One can imagine that the girl cried because she knew there was no joy in their house.

In the morning when she woke, she found Spider sitting alone in the din of an empty diner and he told the girl, "We could no longer live together under the weight of those unfulfilled dreams. She's gone. If you want, the door is open for you to leave as well."

"I've forgotten what it is to be runaway. I don't want that kind of life again."

I believe that Spider smiled, because he got what he truly wanted—the young girl for himself. She would make Spider happy and become his companion. And though she missed Miss Radiance, the girl had a home. No more running away. She had found some semblance of peace.

Still, without Spider's knowledge, the Young Girl would quietly ask about Miss Radiance. People would come into the diner, and she would ask those who may know just what became of her friend. The Young Girl had a letter that she gave to some people with the hope that it would find its way to Miss Radiance. It was a letter to let her know that soon a child was to be born.

I don't know if this is a letter of forgiveness. I don't know if I should say sorry for the life I now have. It doesn't seem fair. I can't help but wonder what you think of me. I can only hope that I am not diminished in your eyes. I don't know if what I really seek is your blessing. If this letter does find you, I hope that you will wish only the best for the child and this family. I would love nothing more than to see you again. Please, if you get this letter, come back home. Until then...

In time, though, the Young Girl turned her thoughts away from Miss Radiance. There was a baby growing strong inside her, but she herself was becoming weak. The Young Girl was bedridden, and Spider called for the Midwife to be by her side at all times.

It is said the baby's arrival came on a night when the moon was shining as brightly as anyone could remember, with stars littering the sky in an abundance never seen before. Spider sat on the front porch steps of his home, and heard the Young Girl's screams pierce the quiet of the night. Spider was powerless to ease her pain. But suddenly the Young Girl's wailing stopped. And what he heard instead was cry of a newborn baby. It is said Spider dropped to his knees and began to weep. When he looked up, he found the Midwife standing solemnly in the doorway. He made a demand, "Tell me about my family."

"It's a beautiful baby boy. You have a son," said the Midwife. "But the girl, I'm sorry Spider, she is gone."

It's not known how long Spider sat on the front porch of his home. But eventually, the Midwife walked up to him quietly and handed him his son. "Here is your child. He is beautiful." It is believed that Spider took the baby and held him limply in his arms. Then he told the Midwife, "You go now. Get the coroner. I'll look after my son."

And when the Midwife left, Spider just sat there with the baby in his arms. Once assured that the Midwife was gone, Spider took his child and headed for the stream out back. It was a long, slow walk. As he made his way to the running brook, Spider sensed someone driving up to his home. Maybe the Midwife returning for something she forgot. Maybe a paramedic. Spider didn't care who it was. He quickened his pace and made his way to the stream. Spider stepped into the stream and wadded through until the water was above his knees. He sensed the presence of footsteps running from the house towards the stream, but he didn't look back. Spider stepped into the stream with the baby. He looked up towards the heavens in anger, then at the son. Spider lowered the baby into the water. And just as he was about to drown his child, a soft, familiar voice quietly said to him, "No, don't."

It was Miss Radiance. "Let me have the child."

It was a miracle that saved the child. It was a miracle that Miss Radiance got the letter; a miracle that she got there in time. It was a miracle that Miss Radiance said to Spider, "Give me the child. He belongs to me now."

Miss Radiance took the baby and returned to her home to raise the boy as her own. And he was loved. Miss Radiance's son grew up strong and healthy in a home that had joy. Still, there were times he had questions, "Why don't I have a father?" The mother told him that in time, she would tell him the truth. And when he was of an age at which he was able to appreciate the abundance of love this mother had shown him, Miss Radiance told him how they came to be in the simplest of ways. "You are a miracle baby; abandoned but saved on the banks of a stream. I saved your life. You saved mine. That's all that matters." The son was able to live with that truth.

Then Miss Radiance's son went off to war.

The son was in The War for a few years when news of his mother's passing made it to the Jungle. He returned home to bury the mother. He was a changed man. There was no change in the awe and reverence he had for the woman who raised him. But he was a man hardened by the horrors he had witnessed in The War. He had seen man's cruel and ignorant ways, and that there was no limit to them. The son returned from The War wanting to know more than just the profound truth of his story—a miracle baby abandoned but saved on the banks of a stream. He wanted to know the whole truth.

There were people who knew his story, those who used to talk in whispers around him—"There's the child Miss Radiance saved from Spider." They would reveal the truth to him. And soon, he too knew the story of the Young Girl, Spider, and Miss Radiance. He heard of the Young Girl who died giving birth to him. He was told of Spider's anger at her death, and how he brought his child down to the stream to drown him.

The son had to meet this man—his father.

The son traveled to the next town over from where he lived. He went to the diner to meet this man—Spider. His father. But the diner was boarded up, no longer in business. So, he went to the home out back, near the stream, where Spider had taken him to be drowned. And he found Spider sitting hunched over in a battered rocking chair on the front porch. The old man was frail and weak. He was barely able to lift his eyes up, as the son approached him. The son gently touched him on his chin to help raise his head so that this man—his father—could see him. The son had a question for the man, "Do you know me?"

Spider looked up with no hint of recognition in his eyes. So the son said, "I'll ask you again, do you know me?"

A long, deep silence filled the time and space that separated them. The son had one hand inside his jacket's pocket, and he could feel the switchblade in his hand. Spider locked eyes with this boy and looked intently at him. Still, there was no recognition in his eyes. But without warning, the son saw the faintest of smiles—a knowing, mocking smile. The son, now angered, pulled his knife out of his pocket and flicked open the blade. Then suddenly, a child's voice called out to him. "Mister, don't you know? Spider don't speak."

The son turned around and saw a little girl no more than seven years old, standing on the porch steps. And he noticed a group of children hopping from one side of the stream's bank to the other. They had come to play in the open field by Spider's home.

"Spider don't speak. And he don't hurt nobody. He lets us play here. Do you know him?"

The son looked at Spider, then at the child, and said, "No, I don't know him."

The Old Man looks over at Hannah, and says, "Knowledge does not free you. I often wonder how life would have been, if I had never been told my own story... if I just lived only off the love of Miss Radiance. I wonder what path my life would have taken, if I hadn't demanded to know the Truth. Knowing the Truth and knowing your history isn't all that it's made out to be."

THIRTY-ONE

I have no image of a father. And so, I dream.

This dream always finds me in a park. Not unlike the one I go to with Mama. But all the swings, slides, and sprinklers are gone. All that remains, the only thing that is recognizable to me, is the tree. It stands tall. It still stands strong, casting out its long, protective branches over the whole playground. Grass and flowers have replaced the concrete plot and steel playthings. In my dreams, my playground is more like a garden.

I see a man standing by the garden's gate. He is gentle looking. He's not very tall, and he is slender. I see a bit of myself in him. We share the same deep brown eyes and long eyelashes.

I ask him, "Do you know me?"

But he is serious and unsmiling. The Guardian dismisses my question, and simply says, "No one can enter."

"Not even me?" I ask.

"No, not even you."

"But this place is meant for a child."

"No, it is not," says this man. "It's meant for those wanting to return home."

I ask him, "Who are you?" I realize that he is in uniform. But a uniform for what, I do not know. "Are you a soldier? Are you here to protect this place?"

"You ask too many questions. Questions that you already know the answers to."

"But you won't let me enter. I ask questions so that I may know why."

"I've already told you why you're not allowed in this place. But you believe that in asking so many questions you will get what it is that you want. You won't accept what you see. You refuse to acknowledge the Truth that is right before you."

I awaken just as the Guardian stiffens and stands straight. I hear Mama say, "It's time to go." We are leaving The River now.

I wake up from my dream. The Guardian will no longer entertain my questions. He says I have the answers. I don't like this dream. But I know it serves a purpose. It lets me know how useless certain questions are. They get you no closer to the Truth. They just distract you from accepting what you see. They distract you from coming to terms with what you know is true. Dreams like this remind me why it is I don't ask Mama about a father. No amount of questions will bring him into existence for me. And so, whatever his story is, it doesn't matter. It has no bearing on how I need to live today. So, I just move on.

THIRTY-TWO

There's a child of Gilead who wakes up in the tiny room of a cramped apartment. He looks over to the bed next to his and finds it empty. An empty bed means only one thing: big brother has yet to return home. The child takes a step out of his bedroom and into the living room. He walks over to a window and takes a peek outside. He sees the emerging light of the morning sun fall softly over an empty and silent courtyard.

The child is not alone, though. A voice comes from the kitchen. He moves towards it, stepping over the fallen sheets and pillows of an unmade pullout bed. The child walks up to the kitchen doorway and sees his mother on the phone. She's a large, distrustful woman, dressed in a worn-out robe. The child nods good morning. The mother keeps talking to the person on the other end of the phone.

He knows better than to interrupt her and ask about his brother. She will only say in disgust, "Tum Tum, please." She has no patience, nor a desire to indulge his questions. Three weeks have passed since the young boy last saw his brother. Usually, when the child asks the mother about the brother, he is met with silence. But the day before, his mother told him that his big brother made a run to see friends down South. She doesn't know when he will be back. "I think he'll be home tonight. I just hope that he's not getting into something trifling."

The child has a little more faith in his older brother, though he doesn't know why. The big brother is basically a stranger to him. A distant figure the child only watches from afar. He looks out his apartment window and watches his brother hanging out on the stone tables and wooden benches that dot the project's open courtyard. Sometimes, he finds his brother on the basketball courts across the street. And sometimes, he watches him on the corner by the neighborhood pool hall. The child sees a brother who seems to have no friends. Every now and then, he sees one or two people come up and talk with his brother. Then these people leave. Sometimes, the brother follows after. Sometimes, he does not.

Sharing a room with a big brother means the child has time alone to spend with him. This time together should make up for an older brother who ignores him whenever he comes home from school or is out riding his bike in the neighborhood. The nods and half-hearted glances can be made up with real talk. The child always eagerly awaits his brother's return home.

But on most nights, the big brother slips into the room like a ghost not wanting to be heard nor seen. And so, the child watches his brother, and sometimes, copies the way he lays on his back with his hands behind his head, just staring at the ceiling. Even in the darkness, the child knows that his big brother is angry. But at what or with whom, the young boy doesn't know. He often asks, "Why are you mad?"

"Niggas fightin' over crumbs. It's just life. Go to sleep."

The child gazes out his window, trying to understand why his brother can't find peace. He can hear his widowed mother in the kitchen still talking on the phone, still spewing venom, "I wish she would... I hate her sorry ass."

And so, the child awakens hungry and remains so because his mother has yet to make time to feed him. He is unable to think too deeply on things for any length of time. But it seems his brother just might be right. "It is just life. You're supposed to be angry." At whom or what, the little boy is too young to know right now.

THIRTY-THREE

The house is quiet. That's to be expected when late morning makes its slow approach to noon. I catch Mama sitting alone in her studio. She is in a familiar pose, sitting on a small stool with a blank canvass in front of her, and that black portfolio book in her lap. Mama is lost in thought. She doesn't notice that I'm peeking around the doorway. I tiptoe away and let her be.

I go into her bedroom and pull open one of her dresser drawers. It is crammed with old necklaces, beaded bracelets, and other costume jewelry that Mama no longer wears. There are no anklets. I sift through the drawer. I notice a little box that looks out of place. It is an empty candy box, and it fits in the palm of my hand. The box is gold. Its tiny lid is sprinkled with little white stars. I take Pretty Girl's anklet and tuck it away inside the box, and put the box in the inner pocket of my shorts. A perfect hiding place.

You can count on one hand, the number of people walking down my block. There are even fewer cars that drive past this way. But from my bedroom, I hear the ping-like sound from the spokes of somebody's pedal bike. And it's racing up and down my block—over and over again. I go to the window to take a look. It's Tum Tum. Figures. He pedals past my window again. He rides slowly. Like he's looking for a house. My house.

I've said it before; Tum Tum is not my friend. I have no clue as to why he's on my block. But I am a friend to curiosity. I head outside and sit on the rail of our front steps. Tum Tum doesn't see me at first. But I see him. I watch as he rides to the end of the block. I watch as he pauses and takes a long look in the direction of the playground. It seems like he's looking to get someone's attention. I don't know. I can't say for sure.

Tum Tum starts back my way. He spots me on my front steps and begins to pedal faster. He's all out of breath by the time he gets to me.

"What's up? I was looking for you. I wasn't even sure you lived down this way."

"What's going on?"

"You still got the jewelry?"

I know what he's asking for, but I play it off and look at him perplexed. "What are you talking about?"

"That little girl's jewelry... that was lost in the park. The diamonds."

"I always have it on me. Why do you ask?"

"I've seen that little girl you said it belongs to."

"You lie."

"No, she's in the park. You'd better hurry, kid."

———

Mama says I can go to the park ahead of her. Mama has no clue as to what I'm up to. She says she'll be close behind. That means I don't have much time. Tum Tum has gone ahead of me, and when I catch up to him, I see him staring at an empty park. Pretty Girl is gone.

"She is on her way back to Gilead. Follow me."

I'm expecting for us to quickly catch up to Pretty Girl. But there is no sign of her. A part of me thinks Tum Tum is up to something. That he's making this all up. But why?

We race down the street and soon come upon my church. I stop. I forget just how close my church is to Gilead. All that separates me from Gilead is a small, no-name discount grocery store, and the open lot of Mama's school's play area. Right on the other side is Gilead.

I tell Tum Tum, "I can't go any further."

Tum Tum doesn't believe me. "What... what are you talking about?"

"I'm not going any further. I can't. I have to get back to the park before Mama gets there."

"You're a baby. Thought you wanted to get the jewelry to the girl?"

"I do."

"Don't seem like it. You're playing mama's boy again."

I am tired of being called a mama's boy. Especially by some little gangsta kid. I won't apologize or feel bad for listening to a mama who cares. A mama with some smarts. A mama who takes an interest in what I do. Tum Tum doesn't know me.

I want to curse him out. But I'm saved from going the way of the world when I hear a voice say, "You heard the young man." It's Pastor, and he's standing in the open doorway of the church. He looks down from the top of the steps. Usually, he has a pleasant way about him and an easy smile. But his look is firm. He has a hardened gaze coming out through narrowed eyes.

Tum Tum takes the L. He's disgusted with me. He grunts and rides off without saying another word. Pastor and I watch him disappear somewhere deep inside the Gilead Complex. I turn to Pastor. His stance softens, and he looks at me with approval.

"I like how you stood your ground. You didn't let yourself be led astray. I'm impressed."

"Just listening to Mama."

The Pastor smiles at the mention of Mama. "How is she?"

I should be on my way, and say, 'Mama's fine.' But that wouldn't be the truth. "She's been better," I say to Pastor. "Mama is in a sad space. I don't think she believes that happiness is real."

Pastor doesn't say anything at first. He considers what I say. "She's come to believe in the lie that happiness is not possible. That happens when the world causes you to doubt and lose your way. We must get her to believe that happiness is possible."

"Do you think you can do that? Do you think you can say some words one Sunday that will bring her back? Maybe say something just for her. Say something that will make her believe again."

———

I make it back to the park just as Mama turns the corner. I wait for her at her favorite spot, the special place where a small wooden bench and a stone table sit securely under the shade of the park's giant oak tree. Mama gives a soft, quiet smile when she sees me. She slips a large satchel off of her shoulder and sets it on the table. Mama opens the bag and begins the meticulous task of taking out her supplies—a large paper tablet, two sets of water-color pencils, and a tin case filled with watercolor brushes. Mama takes out a plastic cup and fills it halfway with water from a bottle. Mama opens her tablet and rips out a piece of paper. Mama begins playing with different color pencils and creates a swatch card. Then, just as quickly as she seemed to start, Mama stops. She sits back and seems to take in the whole park.

"Is something wrong?"

Mama smiles softly. "No. This is just the hard part. Getting ready to paint is easy. Finding the inspiration to create something, that's sometimes a little more difficult."

I look around and I see what I always see—an empty, lifeless park. It's just Mama and me. I tell her, "There's nothing here to inspire you. This is the Dead Zone."

"There's peace and there's quiet," says Mama. "Lessons have been learned right here on this spot. I've seen the worst in people, but I've seen the best, too. Inspiration can be found here. It may not seem like it, but there is beauty in this place."

"Beauty? Then where are the children, Mama?"

"Soon, they'll come," she says. "Soon, they'll come."

THIRTY-FOUR

The Old Man stands under a sycamore tree, one of many that dot the quiet, cobblestone street that runs on the opposite side of the playground. Its heart-shaped leaves cast shadows long enough to keep the Old Man hidden, as he watches the Boy playing in the park from afar. An elderly woman with silver hair tied in a bun emerges from her neatly kept carriage house. With broom in hand, she begins to sweep away the fallen bark that litters the street in front of her home. The woman pauses for a moment and looks up at the Old Man. Her eyes are warm and kind.

"Wonderful, isn't it?'

The Old Man is surprised that the stranger is speaking to him. He examines the woman cautiously. The silver-haired woman doesn't take offense. She offers up a gracious smile. "We appreciate the same thing... children at play."

"It is nice to see," admits the Old Man.

"Reassuring."

The silver-haired woman sweeps the remaining leaves into the gutter. She looks over at the park and the Boy playing on the swings. "This little boy is the only one who ever comes here. I keep asking myself, where have all the children gone?"

"I wish I knew the answer to that, too," says the Old Man.

"Perhaps fear keeps them away. It's easy to become ruled by fear."

"A good parent wouldn't allow their child to be ruled by fear. It will only make them weak."

"You speak the truth."

"I make it a point to come out whenever I see the boy around here. I offer nothing more than another set of eyes to watch over him."

"And to keep that spirit of fear away from him."

"I want him to grow strong with a warrior's spirit. Why do you watch the boy?"

"For the reason we all should... the child gives us hope."

———

There's a cobbler's shop along the Road Less Traveled. It is small and unremarkable, two doors down from a tiny pizzeria. The shop is crammed between a dry cleaner and the neighborhood Laundromat. The painted letters on the glass front door have faded away, making the shop's name impossible to read. But a name is unnecessary. Everyone living along the Road Less Traveled knows this is Pharaoh's place.

The Old Man pauses for a moment at the door. The shop is cluttered and disheveled. There are shoes everywhere. They're on the floor, on workbenches, and on the shelves that line the wall. The Old Man steps in, walks up to the counter located in the rear, and stares towards the back. He keeps a watchful eye on a darkened entranceway peppered by bright lights. The Old Man hears the steady rumble of whirring machines coming from the backroom. But the equipment suddenly goes silent, and a voice calls out from the shadows, "Welcome, friend."

Pharaoh emerges from the unlit entry. A portly and plump-sized man, Pharaoh takes off his dye-splotched apron and tosses it on a nearby counter. He motions for the Old Man to join him in the backroom. Together, the two friends navigate their way through the chaotic den of knives and vats of gluey liquids. Pharaoh's hands are unclean, stained with shoe dye and polish that is hard to remove. Pharaoh foregoes shaking hands, and greets the Old Man warmly with a hug instead.

"I knew you couldn't stay away for long."

"I wanted to come back sooner..." the Old Man's voice trails off.

"But the Lady Dame?"

"Her silence told me the time was not right."

Pharaoh finds two stools and invites the Old Man to sit.

"I kept my word to you. I've kept a watchful eye on Hannah and the child."

"Yes, you have. But I just had to see for myself."

"And are you satisfied?"

"Hannah is a good mother. She is raising the boy well. But I can tell that her spirit is not at peace right now."

"The whole neighborhood knows about her lost student. The little girl from Gilead."

"It's difficult to keep children out of harm's way. We ought to tell God, 'We get it.' That's not a lesson Hannah needed to learn again."

"Is that why you and the Lady Dame left, to escape that lesson?"

"Couldn't face up to being reminded of it every day and every time we saw Hannah."

"But now you're back, hoping to heal old wounds."

"That was the intent. But it seems that I have rattled the serpent instead. And now I must pay to keep it silent."

"He wants how much money?"

"He's a merchant man. He claims I should know how much that silence is worth."

"And do you?"

"I have a figure in mind."

"I know you won't tell me what it is, but I will help you anyway that I can. Just ask."

"What do you know about the shop and what goes on in there."

"There's not much that I can share. You should remember what it looks like inside. It's the same massive square room. But now built for gambling. There's a guard covering the door in the back. He will pat you down. Word has it there are private poker games at night. But I don't know how to get you inside."

"I can gain entry. That's not a problem. Greed will get me in."

Pharaoh looks skeptically at the Old Man. "You know you're always going to be at his mercy. Maybe it's best to allow the truth to come out. It will free you."

"I don't have that sort of faith."

"You will never have enough money to buy off his silence."

"I will convince him that it is enough."

THIRTY-FIVE

"…Ye shall know the Truth, and the Truth shall make you free."

—John 8:32

The Boy saw beside the path, a clump of bushes that were heavy and inviting, with red, juicy berries. He rushed to them and began to pick and eat the sweet, ripe berries. But then he heard a noise. And looking up, he came face to face with a very large and hairy bear. The bear was only a few feet away in the bushes, and himself eating the tasty berries. The boy realized that those large arms were capable of reaching out to catch him and crush the life out of him. And so, he did not move, but stood with the berries still sweet on his tongue, his lips red with juice, his cheeks now white with fright.

But the bear only stared and waited too… for a moment. And then the long, white teeth showed in his fuzzy face, and one massive set of claws moved… and he began to pick and munch more of the ripe berries. The boy, realizing that the bear was hungry only for berries, smiled and began to breathe again, and went back to eating. After several minutes of filling himself, the boy was ready to move along, and, smiling and waving to his friend, he left the bushes and continued on the path.

***

I tell the Old Man, "The story could have stopped there."

"But it didn't. Why do you think it did not?"

"Perhaps God was looking out for the boy. He was being protected. The boy thought the bear would hurt him. He thought the bear would stop him from continuing on his journey."

"But the bear didn't. So, what does that tell you?"

"That maybe we see obstacles that are not really obstacles," says the Boy. "We imagine roadblocks that are not really there. They're just excuses meant to stop us from seeing our journey through."

"And the author knows the story wouldn't be complete if he ended it there."

"But to say a story must have a true ending is not true to life, though. There are a lot of people's whose stories are incomplete and unfinished."

The Old Man smiles at the Boy's wisdom. "Or maybe the question is, what makes a story complete?"

"In school, when I'd write stories, I'd tell my teacher, 'I don't know where my story ends.' And she'd look at me like

I'm crazy. But sometimes, it wouldn't seem right if I forced an ending onto it."

"You just wanted it to go on and on."

"I suppose so."

"But you know, in your heart, that your teachers are right. It can't be that way; a story can't go on forever. There are always endings. People just have problems with endings that don't serve their desires. But don't be fooled. All stories have endings."

THIRTY-SIX

Every summer, Hannah allows herself one day to revel in the Madness. Each year, there's one day when she goes out of her way to join the masses for the Carnival. It's a day when she hides behind a festive mask and slips into the Madness unnoticed. That day is here.

Hannah pulls out a small shoebox from beneath her bed. She opens it and takes out a purple metallic mask with cat eyes. It has a silvery lace overlay design cutout on the top and sides. Gold glitter accents the mask while a sparkling green jewel adorns the top. Hannah takes a long look at herself in the mirror, before putting it on. With her index finger, she delicately traces the black scar on the side of her left eye. She holds it there for a moment, hoping to prevent her eyelid from fluttering ever so gently, and uncontrollably, on its own. Hannah puts the mask on. She toys with it until she is sure that it fits just right. Hannah takes a long look at herself in the mask. She is pleased.

———〜———

Hannah and the Boy get to the parade early, about an hour before the first processions of floats and trucks will snake their way through The Madness. She holds the Boy's hand tightly, and together, they wiggle their way through a deepening sea of people. They find their place near the front, where wooden police barricades cut off access to the street. Hannah glances behind her in search of a familiar face, and sees Chef standing in the open doorway of the Golden Sun. Chef acknowledges Hannah with a nod and a smile. It's the same safe space Hannah makes sure to go to each year right in front of his restaurant. And now, with their spot secure, it's only a matter of time before the parade will begin.

CHAPTER

THIRTY-SEVEN

The Parade makes Mama happy. It always has. It's one of the few times she doesn't seem so serious. It's real joyful, and so you can't help but feel thrilled. We hear the thumping of the bass in the far distance, so we know that the music trucks will be here soon. Women and men are dressed like colorful angels. Some wear colorful animal masks. Even Mama has one on. It looks pretty on her. Mama won't let me wear a mask though. She says I'm too young. Mama says, "You have nothing to hide from."

To be honest, I don't know what the *meaning* of this parade is. I'm not sure Mama knows. And I bet if I were to ask any other grown up, I doubt they would know either. I doubt they even care. Most people just want to be entertained and not have to think about anything important. People are happy. I guess that's all that matters.

Their happiness amps up as an army of half-naked women in Blue Angel costumes approaches us. They're dressed in their feather wings and feathered leg bands, and they strut and twerk and dance alongside a music-pumping truck. Weaving in and out of the army of angels is a trickster—a man dressed in a monkey's mask with large curved teeth. He carries a pole with a calf's tail. He playfully taunts the crowd and dangles the tail in front of people. Slung over his shoulder is a bag full of magic potions and treats. Every now and then he reaches inside and tosses beads or a rabbit foot into the crowd. Mama smiles at the sight of the Trickster but she still holds my hand tight.

Truck after truck, it's pretty much the same thing: an army of angels—sometimes dressed in blue, sometimes in red or purple—pass by. And as they dance and prance before us, there is always a trickster amongst them. But it doesn't get boring. Watching people never gets boring.

But I notice that everybody is pretty much wearing the same thing, just with different- colored feathers or different-colored cat eye masks. And so, I make up a game to play. I start counting all the truly *unique* people at this parade—the ones who *didn't* dress up in costume. I imagine their stories might be more interesting.

I twist and stretch to count as many unique people as I can, but Mama is not letting go of my hand. However, her attention is not really with me. She is looking out into the parade, and at the Trickster, who is making his way towards her. He teasingly shows Mama his bag of tricks. Mama smiles at the Trickster. She gestures towards herself, as if to say, *you have something for me?* The Trickster reaches inside and pulls something out. But he hides it, not revealing what's in his hand. The Trickster tosses it at Mama, and puff... glittery powder floats like little, twinkling stars in the sky. Mama shields herself from the Trickster's magic. She lets go of my hand. I don't bolt away. The sea of people around me acts like a current pushing me gently away from the safety of Mama's grasp. A woman screams, "Nooo... Don't!" A gunshot rings out. *Pop!* I don't see a shooter, and I don't see anyone hit. But still, people are going crazy and begin to run every which way. I stand frozen, about to be trampled. Suddenly, I am swept away in someone's arms from behind. It is Mama. And she races to hide and take cover in the first shop she can find.

THIRTY-EIGHT

The gambling parlor in the backroom of the old candy shop is an expansive room, carpeted in red. An oval, felt-topped table sits in its center, surrounded by ten black chairs. A flat-screen TV is mounted on the far wall, silently rebroadcasting last night's baseball game. Lining the back wall is a trio of slot machines with dancing lights. The room is cut-off from The Madness. And when empty of patrons, like it is now, it is The Merchant's sanctuary, the place where he counts his money.

The Merchant doesn't hear the gunshot. But he hears Fox call to him from the main store, "Boss man. Come check this out." There is urgency in his voice.

The Merchant locks up the money in a small safe on the wall and leaves the shadowy back room. He makes his way out front, annoyed by this distraction, which prevents him from doing something more important. He sees Fox standing near the front door. Fox motions for the Merchant to look towards the corner of the shop. The Merchant can't believe his eyes. Hannah and the Boy are huddled on the floor.

"There was a shooting outside. There was a mad stampede. I let them in."

The Merchant nods and motions to Fox to keep the front door locked. The Merchant then turns his gaze to Hannah and the Boy, who are the only ones in the shop. Hannah's is focused on her son. She hugs the Boy tight, and showers him with kisses, repeatedly asking over and over, "Are you OK...? Are you OK...?"

Fox glances out the window. Chaos remains on the street. Police sirens wail, as cop cars come to a screeching halt not far away. "It's still hectic out there."

Hannah looks up, and for first time, takes notice of her surroundings. She is disoriented and draws the Boy close. Fox extends his hand to help Hannah and the Boy to their feet.

The Merchant continues to study Hannah and the Boy, before finally saying, "Do you know me?"

Hannah is unsure. "No, I don't think so."

The Merchant walks over to the front cash register and opens its drawer. He begins shuffling through some papers stuffed inside. The Merchant pauses to look at a picture that is tucked away in the drawer. He looks over at Hannah and the Boy, and then he turns back to the picture. The Merchant falls deep into thought. He allows for a quiet so deep that it seems to silence the mayhem outside. The Merchant puts the picture back into the cash drawer and closes it. He walks over to Hannah and her child. He kneels down to get a closer look at the Boy. "You're very handsome." He turns to Hannah, "But I'm looking for the resemblance."

"The eyes. He has my eyes."

The Merchant takes another close look at the boy, and then at Hannah, "Maybe so, but I'm not so sure about that. They could be the eyes of his father. The boy doesn't have the scars you have."

Hannah lifts up her mask slightly. "You know who I am?"

"I know your story. That means I know who you are."

"You knew my father?"

"Please, that's a question a child would ask. You've always avoided this place. You never wanted to know me, someone who knew your father."

Hannah looks down at the Boy, "You OK? I think we should go now."

"You're ready to take him back into the world?" The Merchant takes another long look outside. "So much madness."

"So unnecessary," says Hannah.

"Perhaps. Or just part of the grand plan. A necessary evil to weed out the weak."

"Who are you to pass judgment and call out the weak? That sort of arrogance can only lead to ruin."

"Weak, strong—who is to say who is which? Roles change from moment to moment. In the end, everything about life is random. Everything happens by chance. Look how you have found yourself here. The randomness of it. Some believe there's meaning to everything. I'm not so sure of that. But for you to end up here does show what lengths one is willing to go to in order to protect their child. But I think, you, of all people, know just how hard it is to keep children safe and out of harm's way. Your father knew that. You being the teacher for that little girl from Gilead confirmed that for you, too."

The Merchant glances over at Fox and smiles. Fox says nothing, choosing instead to stare down at the floor, distracting himself with a coin that he pushes around with his sneaker. The Merchant's mockery hangs heavy and uncomfortable in the quiet of the shop. It causes Hannah to strengthen her stance.

"You said you know me. You said you know my story. But I think this mask has a way of fooling you."

Hannah slips off her mask completely and looks at it for a brief moment. Then, without hesitation, she tosses it into a trash bin near the Merchant's foot. This surprises the Merchant, who looks up from the trash bin, and finds Hannah staring back at him through narrowed eyes that are trying to bring the truth into focus.

"You see these scars and you think you know my story. You think that you know me. But only the arrogant would believe these are the marks of the weak. Of the sheep. The weak have no scars. Only the strong do. Only those willing to fight have scars. Feel free to ask the person who put mine here."

The Merchant kneels back down to the Boy's eye level. "And where are his scars? Are they unseen? You don't truly believe the words you speak. They're like a good pastor's sermon. Just words to comfort and pacify. You best go back out into the Madness, before the boy learns a little something about who he is."

THIRTY-NINE

The Merchant says, *go back out into the Madness before the boy learns a little something about who he is.*

I don't know this man. But he speaks with authority on things he claims to know about me. He should dress up like one of those jesters from the parade. He's no better than them. He's all about tricks and talking in riddles meant to confuse. There's power in keeping people in the dark.

I know this much though: the Merchant's words have unsettled Mama. She holds my hand tight. We're back on the Road Less Traveled, heading home. We walk slowly and in silence. The commotion from the Madness has vanished. The parade is back on. The shooting is a distant memory. The music and the revelry have started up again. It's almost as if the violence never happened.

Mama's slows her steps and we find ourselves just outside the park's entrance, right by the bench and table Mama always seems to have to herself. As always, no one else is at the playground. She takes a seat and pulls me close to her. She just holds me for the longest time without saying a word. Then she pulls back just a bit and takes a moment to gaze deeply at me. At first, she doesn't say anything. She softly touches my braids until finally, she says, "Be leery of people who say they know you; people who say they know your story. They may know about a few events that have happened to you, but that does not give them the authority to speak as though they know the truth about who you are. It's just a trick to create doubt in your mind."

"How do I fight against people like that? People who claim to know me?"

"You test them. Say to them, 'Prove it. What do you know about me?'"

"How should I expect them to answer?"

"If they really know you, they'll say, 'You are loved'."

As he moved up the path, the boy noticed it was becoming steeper and much harder to travel. And he was beginning to wonder when or how or if he would ever see his wolf, and meet his wolf, and know his wolf, and be able to answer the strange desire he held within himself to feel what the wolf felt deep in the night. Suddenly, he heard a noise. A stone tumbled, and the clatter echoed as the boy froze on the trail. His eyes darted left and right, looking for the source of the movement, when something large moved

*and leaped onto the path. His heart stopped, then it began to beat
again, as he saw the intruder clearly. It wasn't the wolf, but a small
deer—a yearling, a young male—whose nebbish horns were just
beginning to show on the top of his head. The two of them stared at
one another for a moment—curious, fearless, silent.*

*The deer gazed at the boy wide-eyed. The boy gazed back, and
suddenly he was concerned that the yearling might be in danger.
And he spoke quietly to the young deer.*

*"Oh, do be careful here. There's a bear down the path a way.
And a wolf about, I think.*

*I'm searching for that wolf myself, but you? I don't think you
are ready to meet him."*

*The deer stared back in wonder and listened. "Be careful, lit-
tle man. Up here, all alone and so friendly. Be wary of those who
would hurt you."*

———

Be wary of those who would hurt you.

I ask the Old Mann, "How can you tell who is dangerous
and who is not?"

"You just have to accept that they're everywhere. Take no
one for granted?"

I tell the Old Man, "Today we crossed paths with someone
who is dangerous, but Mama showed me something. She's not
afraid of dangerous people. She's willing to stand up to them."

I tell the Old Man how at the parade, we came across the
Merchant, who claimed to know us—to know our story. He

talked as though Mama is not being honest about who we are. That she's hiding the Truth. Or that she's hiding from the Truth. It's confusing. I ask the Old Man, "Why would he talk to Mama that way?"

For the first time, I sense that the Old Man feels troubled. He shifts uneasily. It takes him a while to return my gaze. But finally, he says, "He thinks he's has power over your mama. That he's in control."

I ask the Old Man, "How do you deal with people like that?"

He is not quick to answer, but I sense the Old Man is deadly serious when he says, "You don't meet the havoc they wreck with love. You meet it with force. Through the force of your words, your thoughts, and your might."

FORTY

The Old Man is restless. He lies awake in a room blanketed by darkness. It is a little past one o'clock in the morning, and the silence outside his window is deep. But now he hears footsteps approaching, about a half block away. They eventually stop close to his ground floor window. The Old Man slightly cracks open the curtains. There's a shadow of a man's figure leaning against the front gate. The Old Man reaches for the only security that he has—his razor-sharp switchblade. He flicks it open and then shut. The Old Man slips on his gray, long-sleeved T-shirt and pulls on blue sweatpants. He palms the switchblade into the sleeve of his T-shirt and heads outside.

The Old Man emerges from the bottom steps of his basement apartment and sees the Merchant standing by the front gate.

"What's up, Killer?" says the Merchant, flatly. Then he takes out a Black & Mild cigar and lights it up. He offers it to the Old Man. The Old Man says nothing, so the Merchant keeps it for himself.

"I'm sure you've heard of my encounter today. Made me think it's time I pay you a visit. To make sure that you're taking me seriously. But hey, Killer, I just want to tell you a little story. Do you like stories?"

The Old Man nods, "I do."

"You know what they say about stories? They say that a good story reveals the Truth. Jesus told stories. He knew they were the best way to get people to see the light. He told those parables in order to get people to walk in Spirit and in Truth. I have a good story, Killer."

The Old Man plays along with the Merchant, and asks, "Really?"

"Yes, a love story. You like love stories, Killer?"

"Perhaps... perhaps not."

"There once was a girl and a boy. The girl is pretty and comes from a good family. She has a smile—a bright, brilliant smile—that reflects a faith in the goodness of life. It's a smile inspired by her father. People called him the Candy Man.

"And this father loved his daughter. Sometimes when you visited the candy store he owned, you'd catch the father with his child on his lap and he would be singing a little song off-key:

My Hannah Doll, my Hannah Doll
Oh, how I love my Hannah Doll
I will forever keep you safe and away from harm

"Now, as this little girl got older, she would come back from college each summer and she would help out in her father's shop working the front counter, using her education to help her father with the books. She wasn't aiming to be no accountant, though, because she had an artist's spirit. She wasn't ruled by money and how to take care of it. Many a time during the summer, people would come into the store and they would see the pretty little girl sitting behind the counter working on a sketch or a drawing.

"It was during one of these summers the pretty girl heard the front door swing open. She looked up from her artwork and saw the Kid. He was handsome and strong. But he was from the other side of the tracks... or better yet, the other side of the street, across from the Candy Man's shop. The Kid wasn't from around here either, but he was part of the rough crowd that hung out at that storefront club, Illusions. Like so many of the lost boys who hang out in front of Illusions, the Boss Man—a merchant—took him in. Now this Boss Man wanted to do a little business with the Candy Man. 'The neighborhood is changing,' is what the Boss Man told the Kid. 'Soon a little hole-in-the-wall gangster hangout like Illusions will no longer have a place in this community.' The Boss knew that numbers, gambling, and the drug business needed a new home base. The corner store will always serve that purpose. The Boss tried to get the Candy Man to partner up with him. But the Candy Man had character. He fought in The War and he did things he was ashamed of. So, this was his chance to do right. To make amends.

"But the Candy Man didn't realize, you don't say 'no' to this Boss Man. He wants what he wants. He told the kid, 'You are a stranger to them. Make friends with the girl. See what you can learn about the Candy Man and his family.'

"He was told to act with class and befriend the sweet girl. 'Go in there on a regular basis and charm her. Come across as someone with goals and ambition.

"So the Kid played his part. He was respectful. He took an interest in her artwork. He would see her leave the shop alone and he would time it just right to meet up with her and talk to her as she walked home. And he was smart. It was during the walks home that he told the pretty girl that he would like to meet her away from the store.

"She began meeting him in the park nearby. She'd sneak away for lunch and a movie during the day. The girl kept the affair to herself. She knew what side of the street the boy came from because the girl would watch him. She saw him through her store window, and she saw how the young man would talk to the rude boys hanging out in front of Illusions. And though the young man didn't seem like the hustlers and gangstas from across the way, she knew that her father wouldn't approve. Nor would the Pretty Lady Dame. The girl kept the Kid a secret from them.

"'I think the girl is falling for me hard. What should I do?'

"'You know what's next,' said the Boss.

"But she's not ready.'

"Say, 'I love you'. She's a child. She will accept those silly words as truth. She will give herself to you. She doesn't know how hollow those words are.'

"Then one day the Kid said to the Boss, 'It's happened. She feels violated because I hardly speak to her. And now, she may be carrying my child.'

"'If she comes to you, walk away. Deny the child.'

"And so, it was a summer night, probably a lot like this night—calm, peaceful. The girl told the Kid to meet her at the park. There is news to share. She was frightened. The boy could hear the fear in her trembling voice when she said, 'I am having your child'.

"The Kid did as he was told to do... he rejected the child. And he did it in the cruelest of ways; he simply turned and walked away without saying a word. He left the girl stunned and in disbelief. So, she grabbed him and screamed, 'I won't let you deny this child!'

"The boy was strong, and he pushed her away. But the girl kept coming after him. And so, he hits her. But she's a fighter. She kept coming after him. She punched, scratched, kicked him. But the Kid was strong, and he hit her again... and again until she had no more fight in her. And this boy, who said those hollow words—'I love you'—left the girl in a huddled mess beneath some battered, old park bench. The boy walked away from the girl and the child to come."

The Merchant stops speaking. He turns his cold, steely eyes on the Old Man, searching for some reaction to his story. But the Old Man offers him no satisfaction. He sits impassively. The Old Man breaks the silence with a simple question, "Are you done?"

The Merchant tells the Old Man that he is not.

"Because you see, I lie. This is not really the love story of a girl and a boy. Rather, it's about a man's love for a family and the steps he'd take in order to protect that family's honor. That Kid and the Boss Man never gave much thought to this man, who sat in the shadows watching from the back of the candy shop. Everyone thought this man's life was insignificant. Sure, little kids were afraid of him. But to adults, he was a sorry old man who was nothing more than a floor sweeper, living off the kindness of a friend. No one knew what kind of man he was. No one knew what this man was capable of... except for the girl's mother. The mother knew that her husband, the old solider, wasn't capable of avenging their daughter and restoring her honor. It is believed that she went to this man, who sat in the shadows, and asked, 'Can you make it right?'

"This man assured her that he could. But the Kid and the Boss Man never gave a thought to the possibility that they would be punished for their evil. They didn't know that there are still men out there who are the shepherds of children. Righteous men fueled with enough anger to seek out revenge.

"And so the Kid... vanishes. He is never heard from again. A body never even turns up. The Kid simply no longer exists.

"In time, the girl heals... well, except for the scar that remains by her eye. She doesn't know what happened to the Kid she once loved but who denied their child. The mother, Pretty Lady Dame, goes back to the island where she is from. The father dies—I guess, you can say—from a broken heart from knowing he failed to protect his child. And the guardian angel, that blessed man who is the protector of children, slips back into the shadows. And everything is right with the world."

The Merchant looks up at the Old Man and tries to read his expression. The Old Man reveals nothing. This seems to give the Merchant pleasure. "I've waited ten years to tell that story, Killer. Ten years to tell *your* story. But this is not a fairy tale. No one gets to live happily ever after. You don't get the chance to run away from the Truth."

The Old Man asks a simple question, "What is it that you want?"

The Merchant takes out a photograph and holds it up to the Old Man. "I want to know what happened to the Kid in the picture. The Kid in this story. I want to know where the body is."

"And if I don't tell you?"

"Then little Hannah and child will learn from me what you truly are... Killer. I know you can't live with that. As I've said before, you will pay and tell me what it is that I want to know. And you will admit to me what you really are."

The Old Man sits awake in his room and remembers...

The soldier walks up to the candy shop and finds the gate drawn down halfway. He slips underneath and enters the store. There are no lights on. He walks towards the storeroom located in the back of the shop. A gentle tap on the door is enough to open it. The soldier hears a voice. It's low and unsteady. From the darkness, this voice calls out a simple question, "How far will you go to protect your child?"

The soldier sees the shadow of the Candy Man, as he sits on a battered metal chair in the din of this back parlor. The Candy Man waits for an answer. But the soldier remains silent and reaches to turn on a light.

"Leave it off," says the Candy Man.

The soldier does as he is told. He pulls out another chair and takes a seat across the room from his friend.

"You didn't answer my question," says the Candy Man.

"It's not really a question of how far one would go to protect a child. You're asking, how far will I go to get retribution."

"You've seen what was done to Hannah. You have seen the crime. She's scarred for life. Hannah will never be able to look at me the same through that battered eye."

The soldier does not answer.

"I know the Pretty Lady Dame has come to you. She believes that I am weak. She doesn't think I can make this right."

"And I can?"

"You once admitted to being a Hunter."

"And you were one too."

"No, I never was. All I had to do was pilot a boat and watch silently from the shadows. I was never a hunter. It's not who I am."

"But you told me that I couldn't stay the Hunter forever."

"And wasn't it you who said, 'You can't transcend what you are?'"

The soldier does not say anything. He studies his friend and knows this much is true: Candy Man is powerless to protect the honor of his own child.

The soldier tells his friend, "As I've told your wife, I will do what you're unable to do. I will hunt down the people who did this to your child. I will find the ones responsible, no matter how long it takes. And when they see me, they will know fear. They will come to fear me and by extension, they will fear you, too. And they will know there are no victims here. They will know their kind doesn't win."

This is the last conversation the soldier has with his friend. In less than a week's time, the Pretty Lady Dame knocks softly on the soldier's door, and calmly tells him, "He is gone. Your friend went quietly in his sleep... without a fight." And with no hint of a waver or tremble in her voice, the Pretty Lady Dame tells the soldier, "You know what must be done."

<hr />

It will be simple. The soldier knows who he is looking for. It is the Kid, the one who hangs out across the street in front of *Illusions*. It is the slick-looking Kid he has seen coming into the store every so often to talk to Hannah. The soldier is sure of this.

The soldier knows that it is not a question of *who* the Kid is, but rather one of *where* the Kid can to be found. He no longer hangs out in the street. He hasn't been seen in a while. So, the soldier asks himself, "What stands out about him?" The answer is easy: the Kid is always pressed and clean. His clothes always match. His hair is immaculately cut with a hairline that is razor sharp and neat. The Kid's pencil thin mustache is always neatly trimmed. The Soldier bets the Kid can be found at the barbershop.

There is a neighborhood spot that the young boys from Illusions go to get their cuts. It is a drab, non-descript parlor four blocks north of the Candy Man's store. The soldier knows this is the place he'll find the Kid. So, he camps out across the street from the shop. From the moment it opens to the time it closes, the soldier comes around every hour and leans on a pole across the street and watches to see who comes in and out of the shop. From his perch, the soldier stares deep inside to see who is sitting in the barber chairs. The soldier is patient.

After seven days, the Kid reveals himself. He comes early to the shop. It is mid-morning, in the middle of the week and there is only one barber inside. No one else is around. This is the way the Kid probably wants it. The boy doesn't seem to have a care in the world. The soldier watches him smile and laugh with his barber. This Kid has already forgotten what he has done to Hannah.

When the Kid is done, he quickly leaves the shop. The soldier follows him. It turns out he only lives two blocks east of the barbershop. It is an old, red brick building—a four-story walkup—with an old fire escape painted black, hanging off the front.

As the Kid enters the building, the soldier turns his gaze towards the windows. He is looking for any movement—the opening of a window, the tussling of curtains... anything. After a few minutes, the soldier sees a hand fumbling with the blinds to a fourth-floor apartment. This must be where the Kid lives.

The soldier goes home and prepares as a hunter would. He takes out his switchblade and sharpens it. The soldier then takes out a pair of black gloves and snaps them on tight to make sure they fit properly. The soldier comes back the next morning and finds a quiet spot across the street from where the Kid lives. But it's the apartment building next door that he approaches.

The soldier acts as though he is searching for his keys when a woman coming out of the building holds the door open for him and lets him inside. He walks up the four flights of stairs unseen. There's a door to the roof that has a latch that easily slides open. He unlocks it and heads outside. The two buildings are connected, so the soldier is able to hop over from one roof to the other. He peeks over the ledge, down to the street below. The block is quiet and empty. The soldier carefully steps down to the fire escape below. Quickly, he begins to tug at the window. It slides open with little effort. The soldier slips inside the apartment. He lands in the kitchen and takes out his knife.

The kitchen is small and neat. There are only two unwashed glasses in the sink. The soldier walks softly into the next room. It's the living area. A blanket covers the couch and a bed pillow lies fallen at its legs. An empty beer bottle stands alone on the coffee table. Music from the radio plays softly in another room. The soldier follows the sound. He walks up to the door and gently taps it open. There is no one inside. The radio beside the bed has been left on. The soldier goes to the check the bathroom. It is empty. No one is home.

The soldier looks in a hall closet and ruffles through the few shirts and jackets hanging inside. Eyeing the varying sizes of the clothes—some large, some extra-large, a few double- extra-large—the soldier concludes two people are staying in this apartment. But the place seems more of a hideout than a home. Nothing personal seems to be here. There are no paintings or pictures on the walls. There's not even a pile of mail lying around. The soldier goes back into the kitchen and begins rummaging through the cabinets and beneath the sink. He goes into the bedroom and looks under the bed and finds three shoe boxes full of new sneakers. The soldier begins poking around another closet, which is practically empty. There are a few shirts hanging inside and a few pairs of jeans folded neatly atop a shelf. The walls in the apartment are bare. The soldier goes into the bathroom and opens up the cabinet under the sink. Among the soap and cleaning supplies, the soldier notices a shoebox tucked away in the back. He pulls it out and opens it. There is a 9 mm handgun inside. He pulls out the cartridge. The clip is fully loaded. The soldier puts away his knife and takes the gun with him. He heads into the living room. There are two matching sofa seats at each end of the couch. The soldier pulls them out to the center of the room. He has them facing each other. The soldier goes over to the lamp and unscrews the light bulb. He tests to see if it turns on. It does not. He then takes a seat in the sofa that's now facing the front door. He keeps the gun in his lap. The hunter waits.

⁓

A full moon hangs low amid a starless night sky. The soldier hears the rustling of keys. The door opens and a figure steps into the dark apartment and locks the door behind himself. The figure walks into the living room and turns on the lamp. The light does not come on. The Kid drops the bag that he is carrying and examines the bulb. He screws it in tight and tries again. The light turns on. The soldier sees that it's the Kid, the one who has harmed Hannah. The Kid sees the soldier sitting in the chair pointing a gun at him. He lets out a soft gasp. Then he looks back at the door behind him. The Kid knows he can't run. He turns his nervous eyes back to the gun pointed at him. The soldier nods at the bag on the floor. "Toss it over here."

"It's... it's only food." The Kid does as he is told and tosses the bag at the soldier's feet. He examines the bag to see if the Kid is telling him the truth. There are chicken wings and French fries inside.

The soldier tells him, "Have a seat." He points at the chair directly across from him.

The Kid does as he is told. The soldier studies him. The Kid is smallish and thin. The soldier thinks to himself, "*he is just a child*." The Kid has round shoulders that are hunched in fright. His head hangs low and his gaze is cast downward. The Kid trembles in his seat. "Look at me," says the soldier, quietly.

The Kid lifts his head up. He has what can almost be considered fragile features. He has flawless skin and his eyes are small, yet dark. That's where the evil lies. It's behind the eyes. The soldier has a question for the young man, "Do you know me?"

The Kid looks directly at the soldier. "Yes, I know you."

"Then you know why I'm here."

"Yes," says the Kid.

"And why is it that?"

"You're here because of Hannah."

The soldier's eyes narrow and he stares hard at the young man. He is not satisfied with an answer that is not complete. "Excuse me?"

"You're here because of what I did to Hannah."

That's what the soldier wants to hear. The Truth. The soldier gets up from his chair and walks behind the Kid and places the cold barrel of his gun against the back of the Kid's skull.

"Your name. Tell me your name."

The Kid resists. The soldier presses the gun against the back of the Kid's head a bit harder. He repeats softly. "Tell me your name."

The soldier leans over and waits for the Kid to do as commanded. The Kid finally relents and whispers his name into the soldier's ear. The soldier nods in approval. Then he tells the Kid, "I will speak the truth to you. That person dies tonight."

***

The memory of the Kid fades away, and the Old Man imagines peeking through the window blinds and seeing the Boy sitting patiently on the front steps. Storytime has arrived. But the Old Man waits and, as he often does, studies the Boy from afar. The Old Man has come to realize that all it takes is a glimpse of the Boy at just the right angle, and he sees the Boy's father. The Old Man wonders if his journey is meaningless; if it's just some quixotic quest to uphold a schoolboy's notion of justice. But the Old Man doesn't allow such a thought to linger because he knows that this is how evil does its work. It sneaks in and creates doubt. Doubt in those who seek to hold evil accountable. It is in these moments of silence and stillness that the righteous let evil slip out of their grasp and into that quiet space that always leads to forgiveness.

The Old Man assures himself he will not allow that to happen.

FORTY-ONE

I know where grown-ups hide the truth. They hide it in silence. The truth is tucked away somewhere in Mama's lost and distant gaze. The Old Man conceals the truth behind knowing smiles that take the place of answers to my questions. They don't want me to know the things that they know. But that's OK. That means the truth is something for me to learn on my own.

⁓

Mama is hiding away in her studio. I peek around the corner of the door. Mama can't see me, but I can see her. She sits on the floor with her legs crossed. She is huddled over and curled up with the black portfolio in her lap—the little girl's portfolio. The little girl from Gilead.

"Mama," I say, softly. "Mama." But she doesn't answer.

Mama is lost to me. So I go outside. Besides, it is almost storytime. The Old Man will be coming out to join me soon. I am thankful for his company.

———— ⌣ ————

The Boy noticed the darkening sky and the cold chill of the deepening night air, as it gathered about him. He continued along the bare path, trying not to look too far to the left or the right, trying to keep his footing; wondering if he had been wise in coming here, if he had been right in seeking the wolf in such a lonely and desolate place. He was growing more unsure of himself with each step, as he moved carefully and slowly up the path. Suddenly, he saw something... no, he felt something up ahead. It might have been nothing. It might have been a shadow crossing the moon. It might have been everything he sought.

His heart beat faster. His head grew light, but his eyes stayed sharp, as he stared up the trail. He waited quietly for another sign, and soon came his reward, as the shadows moved up ahead and became living and breathing flesh. There on four paws, eyes reflecting his own bright gaze, head still as stone and pointing down the trail toward him, was the wolf.

The Boy could not move. The red eyes, the great tongue, the huge claws flashed in his memory. But as he stared, he saw none of them. He could also recall the song that had drawn him here, the singer from that distant night now only yards from him, breathing in the cold night and exhaling hot steam.

And as he stood, peering into the wild eyes before him, remembering that sad, sweet song, he felt his heart soften and his fear evaporate.

His eyes filled, and without warning, he knew why he had come here. He knew in that instant what he had traveled to find, what he had heard in that song, what he had embraced in his lonely bed as he had lain awake, listening and wanting. He knew that the song had been a cry for an end to solitude. The cry was to banish loneliness. It had reached out across the miles and the years and touched him. And it had guided him. He knew this now.

And so, with his heart full and his eyes afire with understanding, the boy faced the wolf and he spoke back—with his smile. And in that instant, the two—boy and wolf—were one heart.

"The mystery behind the big, bad wolf has been solved," I say to the Old Man.

"And how was the hero of the story able to solve it."

"He went in search of the wolf. He went after it."

"What does the hero learn from his search?"

"Being willing to seek out the wolf, the boy learns that the beast was not something to fear."

"Why is this important?"

"If the boy only accepted another person's word, he would not have known the truth. He would only believe what others told him to believe about the wolf. Instead, he was able to go through his own experience to understand and know who the wolf is. He learned to live without fear."

"Do you think the wolf reveals himself in the same light to everyone who seeks him out?

I don't answer quickly. "I suppose it depends on what's in each seeker's heart. It depends on what they really hope to find. The seeker can choose to define the wolf however he wants when he finds him. Good. Evil. Both. It's up to the seeker."

The Old Man smiles at me.

"Should I continue the story? I'm almost finished."

The Old Man says I don't need to go on. "There's always tomorrow."

I want the Old Man to tell me the truth, so I ask, "You're leaving soon, aren't you?"

"Yes," says the Old Man. "I can't stay here forever."

"Why not? This could be your home."

"If I stay, I'll just end up disturbing the peace that you and your mother have here."

"You're just saying that to be nice. If you really believed that you'd disturb our peace, you wouldn't have come back in the first place."

"Sometimes selfishness comes with old age. I've become an old man who has become too stubborn to let certain questions go unanswered."

The Old Man says nothing more. Mama is calling for me. I am wanted inside.

"You better go. You're needed."

FORTY-TWO

"The light shines in the darkness, but
the darkness has not understood it."
—John 1:5

After midnight, the front door to the candy shop is locked and the metal gate is drawn down and shut tight. For Fox, his only way inside is through the rear door located in the back alleyway, where a huge, prison-built Goliath stands on night watch. It's the Merchant's other gatekeeper, the one they call Me-Too. Me-Too's only responsibility is to stand silent, look mean, and, if any trouble is to arrive, be quick on the draw with the 9 mm gun tucked away in the belly folds along his waistband. But Fox has no fear of Me-Too. He's a generation older than Fox and is a source of amusement. Fox enjoys finding new ways to be humored by the slow-witted giant. So, Fox rolls up the sleeve of his sweatshirt and shows off a watch.

"Hey, my man, look. I just got this Rolie."

The hulk on guard takes a quick look at Fox's wrist. But not to be outdone, he rolls up his sleeve, and shows Fox an old watch. "Me, too. I got a Rolie. Mine is nicer."

Amused, Fox just shakes his head and thinks, *somethings never get old.* Me-too is oblivious and opens the door. The back room is ghost-quiet, except for the soft hum emanating from an old a/c unit that hangs on a corner wall. The Merchant sits at a table in the center of the room with three other men. Fox ducks in stealthily but can't evade the critical stares of the men at the table. Fox acknowledges one of the men, Shivers, with a subtle point in his direction. He's a spindly man of middle-age with shifty, ferret-like eyes. Next to him, is a slightly younger man, just on the cusp of middle age. He is smartly dressed in a button-down shirt and slacks. He is studious looking, with alert and attentive eyes behind owl-shaped, wire-rimmed glasses.

"What's up, Books?"

"All is good," he tells Fox.

Fox takes a seat at an empty spot at the head of the table. To his right, is a man not known to him. He's a stranger, one with a small oval head, ill-fitted for his broad-shouldered frame. The black circles under his dark, solemn eyes hang like bruises that will never fade. The stranger has anchored his attention on Fox, studying the young tough as though seeking some sort of recollection.

Fox asks the Merchant, "What's up with your man? This dude is looking at me like I've done something to him."

"Trigger doesn't like it when people are late. Just deal," says the Merchant.

Fox takes out several decks of new cards, breaks their seals, and spreads them out across the table for everyone to see. Trigger looks over at the Merchant, and sucks his teeth in disgust. "I thought we were waiting on a real dealer. I didn't come here to have your son hand out cards."

A dark shadow falls across the Merchant's eyes and he chooses to stay silent long enough to allow the quiet to make the men at the table worry. Then in a voice low and emerging from some place dark within, the Merchant says, "He's not my son."

"Sometimes, people don't know, Boss Man" says Books. "You don't make babies."

"Books' gotta lot of nerve," stutters Shivers. "He ain't got no kids himself. None of us do."

The Merchant looks past everyone at the table. He's not listening to them. It's Me-Too's attention that he wants. The big man assures the Merchant that he's taken an interest in what's happening at the table. Me-Too asks a simple question, "We have a problem, Boss?"

"Do we?" the Merchant asks the table.

Trigger shoots a disgusted glance at the Merchant but relents. "We have no problem with your boy dealing cards."

"I didn't think so," says the Merchant. "Deal them up, Fox."

The darkness of the night deepens, and Fox senses a disquiet slipping into the parlor. It is to be expected at this late hour. He swings a nervy gaze towards Trigger. Nothing has changed. The weight of this stranger's probing stare remains. Shivers fidgets with his cards, using his slender fingers to flip up the edges of the dealt cards. He repeatedly peeks at them to make sure he is reading them right. At the far end of the table, Books has a mound of winning chips in front of him, and he jiggles a handful of them. He blinks owlishly, and stares at his cards impassively. No worries.

Fox keeps an eye on the Merchant too. He watches him slip into the shadows often, only to quickly re-emerge time and time again with bottles of beer, vodka, and rum in hand.

"Looking to keep us juiced up," says Books. "Trying your best to separate us from our money?"

Books' words go unchallenged as there's a sudden movement at the back door. Rarely do new players enter the game at this hour. The knock on the door is a cause for pause.

Me-Too takes a hard glance at the video monitor on the intercom. "Hey Boss Man, check this out. We have company. It's that Old Man."

The Merchant says nothing. Instead, he pours drinks for the men at table. It is only after the final glass is full that the Merchant nods his approval for Me-Too to unlock and open the door. The Old Man is ushered in, and immediately raises both hands into the air. He allows himself to be patted down. "I come in peace."

The Merchant gestures towards an empty chair at the table. "Why are you here?"

"I just want to show you that I have legitimate means to do business with you." The Old Man reaches into his pocket and pulls out a handful of bills. "Deal me in? I promise I won't spend it all."

The Merchant studies the Old Man for a moment, and wonders, *is he serious?* But he soon motions to Fox to include him in the next hand. The Merchant takes the Old Man's money and hands him a small stack of chips.

All eyes are on the Old Man. But he reveals nothing. The Old Man keeps his head down, counts his chips, and calmly waits to be dealt his cards. Trigger sits back in his chair, folds his arm, and studies the Old Man suspiciously.

"Hey, Boss Man, where do I know this dude from?"

"Why don't you ask him?"

Trigger turns to the Old Man. "I know you, don't I?"

The Old Man remains silent.

"You don't speak?

The Old Man waits a moment. "Not to people I don't know."

"Books, don't he look familiar?"

"A little bit. But don't ask me no questions. I'm trying to win some money."

"Where you from?"

The Old Man allows Trigger's question to hang in the air. Unnerved, Trigger turns to the Merchant for guidance. But the Merchant offers no answers—he just throws a devilish grin back at him. He is enjoying this time to study the Old Man. Trigger presses on.

"You from here? Or used to be?"

The Old Man doesn't say anything. He examines his cards and throws a chip into the center of the table. Finally, the Old

Man turns to Trigger, and says, "Yeah, used to be. That was a different time and space."

Trigger puffs out his chest, "Finally got you to speak. But I like how you say that, 'a different time and space.'"

The Old Man calls and wins his first-hand.

With a pause in play, Trigger turns his attention back to Fox. "And what about this young cat? I've been trying to figure it out all evening. Now I realize what it is. I've been going back in time with him, too."

Fox stiffens his posture, and reaches for a voice of menace and threat, "How you figure?"

"You remind me of a kid from long ago."

The Old Man looks up from the table, his eyes clocking the presence of this stranger. He is taking him more seriously now. Trigger playfully spins around in his chair. "Hey Boss Man, whatever happened to that kid? He just stopped coming around."

The Merchant speaks in a strong whisper, "Don't talk about the Kid."

"I'm just saying, this cat here reminds me a lot of that kid."

Fox glares at Trigger, "Nigga, you don't know me. Don't put me in your story."

If you know what's good for you, you'll stop talking."

"Oh shit. He ain't like that other one." Trigger makes a sweeping, mocking gesture and pretends to be sizing up Fox for a picture. "I see a little violence behind those pretty-boy eyes."

Then Trigger turns to the Old Man. "Do you know who I'm talking about? Were you here around the time of the Kid? I bet you were."

The Old Man says nothing. Trigger seeks answers from the Merchant.

"That kid was like a son to you. Was to be your legacy. This young cat here is just taking his spot."

"You just don't listen." The Merchant lifts his beer bottle by its neck. He takes a long swig, then pauses to savor its taste. He throws a knowing glance over to Me-Too. "I love this beer."

There's a subtle shift in Me-Too's stance at the door. He appears to be adjusting his seat on the high stool. No one pays attention to his growing shadow as he slithers closer to the card table. Me-Too slinks up from behind and delivers a blow across the stranger's windpipe. Trigger reels back in his chair and crashes to the floor.

"I told you," says the Merchant. "'Don't talk about that kid.'"

"Sh... sh... shit, man. You were warned," stutters Shivers.

Trigger stays huddled on the floor trying to speak. Not in words, but in grunts and high-pitched squeals like those of air wheezing out of a dying balloon. His wails fall on deaf ears. The Old Man looks around and sees that is no one is making an effort to help him up.

"Leave him," orders the Merchant. "He'll be alright."

The Old Man disregards the Merchant and extends a hand to help Trigger to his seat. Me-Too and his large shadow move away from the table. The returning light, though muted and hazy, illuminates the Merchant's soulless eyes—eyes that grab hold of everyone at the table, demanding their presence at his performance.

"You don't know me. None of you do. I'm sitting at a table surrounded by a bunch of broken old men who think of children and legacy only because it's been denied them. And so, you think I'm one of you." The Merchant directs his hardened glare at Fox. "I don't care about nobody's children. Think I give a damn about a little hood rat beyond what he can do for me?"

"Oh, so that's how it is?" asks Fox, with great effort to mask the hurt.

"Yeah, that's how it is."

Fox tosses the cards onto the table. "Shit's getting crazy. Liquor is talking for you. I'm out. Let Me-Too deal."

"Me-Too watches the door. That's his job. You deal. That's your job. Keep your ass put. You don't leave until I tell you that you can leave."

Fox says nothing. He drops the cards and pulls his chair away from the table. Fox doesn't look the Merchant directly in the eye. He just lowers his glare. A rage is building inside of Fox until finally he looks up and challenges the Merchant's authority. "There's something I've been meaning to ask you for long time, Boss Man... Who the fuck is you?... You think I'm supposed to be scared, just because you got some simpleton nigga at the door holding a gun? You think you're unique? You're just a sorry old man running a half-ass gambling parlor. Shit, nigga, you're a dinosaur. I don't need your blessing to go home."

The Merchant doesn't do anything at first, choosing instead to shake his head, and say, "You know this boy's story. His father worked for me. You know him."

Books says, "Yeah, that cat..."

"You don't say his name!" shouts Fox. "You don't talk about him!"

The Merchant laughs him off. "His father was the educated kind. Had that collegiate air about him. The type who brought a sort of respectability to my affairs when needed. He couriered for me, was a peddler to the college crowd down the road and found me high rollers for games. He did whatever I told him to do. But he started flexing and talking about how he wanted to go it alone. But I told him there's no leaving me. His father thought he had smarts and that he could weaken me by stealing from me. He thought it would be easy to part me from my money. Dude forgot I live to count my money. Never going to be a penny short."

Fox lunges across the table to get at the Merchant. But Me-Too jumps in and forces him back into his chair with a strong forearm blow to his chest. Me-Too puts Fox in a chokehold and forces him to look at The Merchant.

"I had your father in this exact same position. The only difference was he was begging for his life. Pleading with me. Asking me, 'What can I do to make it right?' Like he'd ever be able to pay back what he stole. But he promised that he could truly pay me back."

'I'll pay anything.'

'Anything?'

'Yes, anything.'

'Your son. I'll take your son. He becomes mine now.'

"And this father, who had grander ambitions for his son than a cheap, insignificant life in the streets, said, 'Yes, you can have my son.' And so, this bright boy, a good student, who always did as he was told at home, became mine."

Fox struggles to get away from Me-Too's grip. But he can't. "Remember me coming to school with your father. You no longer went home right after your classes were over. Just came with me and hung out with us at Illusions and allowed me to expose you to this world. After only a few years' time, you dropped out school and turned yourself into nothing more than a common hood rat... no future. Your mama couldn't control you anymore. You were lost to her. Your father was ashamed of what he had done. And so, what did he do, Books?"

With a newly revealed truth, Books somberly says, "One to the temple. Damn. Never knew the story behind it."

The Merchant pulls his chair nearer to Fox, and leans over, as though he's whispering in his ear. But he looks directly at the Old Man. "You know the best way to weaken a man who steals from you? Or a man who tells you, 'no.' You don't go at him directly. You don't go after his woman. If you want to weaken a man, you go after his children."

Fox struggles to break free from Me-Too, but he can't. He can barely breathe. He's being choked. The Merchant reaches with his free hand down into Fox's waistband and pulls out a black revolver. "Look at this old shit. Out of all the guns you have locked up at home that I've given you, this is the one you bring to the job."

The Merchant empties the revolver of its bullets and lets them fall to the table. He picks one up and places it in the chamber and spins it. "Sometimes, to make a point though, you gotta get nasty. Gotta get your own hands dirty. Make people know who's the boss."

The other card players nervously pull their chairs away from the table. Shivers stammers, "Oh, shit, man."

"Nobody move," shouts The Merchant. "This show ain't over!"

The Merchant points the gun at Fox's temple. "You ask me, 'who the fuck is you?' I'll tell you who the fuck I am... I'm your God! Say it!"

Fox refuses to answer. He struggles to break free. The Merchant pulls the trigger. Click. Nothing.

"I'll ask you again... who am I?"

Fox still refuses to answer. The Merchant pulls the trigger again. Click. Nothing again.

"Who am I?"

The Old Man says with force, "Answer him."

"You're my God!" answers Fox.

The Merchant leans back in his seat. Me-Too slams Fox face down onto the table. The Merchant hands Fox a cloth. "Here."

Fox takes it and begins to pat his swollen lip. And as he does, the Merchant tells him, "Now, you can go home. You are no longer needed here." Me-Too has the door already open for Fox. He mockingly gestures that the path is clear. Fox gets up slowly and limps to the door. He leaves the Madness without looking back.

Trigger is visibly shaken, he stutters, "You... you... you were just playing right? You palmed that bullet, didn't you?"

The Merchant raises the revolver and points it directly at the Old Man. He takes aim at him. The Old Man doesn't flinch. Then, slowly, the Merchant turns the barrel away and hands the gun, handle first, to the Old Man. The Old Man opens up the chamber and turns it upside down. A bullet falls out.

"What the hell?" Shivers is frantic. "You're crazy! You could have killed that kid!"

The Merchant doesn't take his eyes off of the Old Man, who gets out of his seat to leave. The Old Man stops at the door and looks back at the Merchant impassively. "I'll be back with the money in a couple of days."

"Good," says the Merchant. "I think I've shown you not to say 'no' to me."

FORTY-THREE

It's Sunday. But something strange is happening. I don't get a wake-up nudge from Mama. I wake up on my own. I get out of bed and search for her. She's not in her bedroom, nor the bathroom, nor the kitchen. Neither is she in the living room, where we spend the Quiet Hour. I find Mama in her solitary place. She's up in her studio.

Mama is sitting by her easel, staring at an open, black portfolio—the one with the little girl's work inside. Mama sees me at the door wiping the sleep from my eyes. She closes the book. Mama tells me, "We're not going to church today."

Mama says it like it's not a big deal. Like it's something that's to be expected. I watch her pull the little girl's work out of the portfolio and place it in an envelope. Mama turns her glance to the door where I stand. She tells me to get dressed. Mama says, "We're going out."

I peek out my bedroom window and look up towards the sky. I see gloomy, gray clouds that hang low, barring the sun from sharing its light. It will be only a matter of time before the skies open up and the rains come pouring down. There's a storm headed this way.

Mama gets ready in no time. She's dressed like a little kid with her baseball cap, college sweatshirt, and jeans. Mama is carrying the large envelope. She places it inside her knapsack, and quickly throws the bag over her shoulders. Mama starts off down the street without saying a word. I follow her on my bike. I don't know where it is we're going. Mama hasn't told me.

We pass the playground. I pause to see if Pretty Girl is there. I have her anklet tucked away deep in my pocket, in the small, emptied-out box of candy. But Pretty Girl is nowhere to be seen. Neither is Tum Tum. The park is deserted as always. Mama and I keep walking.

Our church is just up ahead. I hear faint shouts of praise coming from inside. The people are singing. I hear the steady beat of drums and the clash of cymbals. It sounds like a party. I can't seem to remember a time when Mama and I were not part of this celebration. It feels weird not being inside the church on a Sunday. Mama and I say nothing as we walk past. The joyful sounds eventually fade away.

As Mama and I continue down the path away from our church, I can see that the Tower of Gilead is getting closer. The nice brownstone homes lining the street give way to a small supermarket, and then a school—Mama's school. The school is three-stories high and faces out to an open courtyard. There is no playground like they have at my school. A wide, two-lane street separates the Gilead Houses and its apartments from the school and its courtyard. Not many cars flow this way, nor are there many cars parked along the street. At the near end of this two-lane street is a construction lot. Three brick buildings rise amid the rubble.

I tell Mama that I never knew they were building new homes out this way. Mama says it's just the beginning. "They'll be tearing down the Gilead Houses soon to make way for condos."

"Where will all the people go," I ask.

Mama says she doesn't know. She says sadly, "When it comes to the poor of this world, nobody seems to really know or care."

"We're going to Gilead, aren't we?"

Mama nods yes, and points to the Tower of Gilead at the far end of the street. I ride off slightly ahead of her. But she can see me. I have not ridden so far off that she has to be concerned. There's long, narrow path that leads to the Tower of Gilead. The pathway leading to the building opens up into a roundabout, before it narrows again into a slender walkway leading to the apartments. In the center of the roundabout is a dirt-strewn garden. No flowers grow here. There's just a limp, dead tree at its center. Wooden benches, many broken, circle the pathetic plot of land.

As I speed along this path, I hear a voice that is familiar. A voice that's deep, almost harsh. It says to me, "Are you lost?"

I stop and look up. Fox is sitting on the backrest of one of the broken benches. I was so in my own little world that I hadn't even noticed him.

"You look like you're surprised to see me. I'm from Gilead, remember."

"Shouldn't you be at the candy shop?"

My question seems to hurt. It causes Fox to look away with a lost gaze. Fox answers quietly, almost to himself, "You won't see me there no more." But clarity comes back quickly, and he asks me, "But why are *you* here?"

"I'm with my mom." I point to Mama, who's making her way up the path towards us. Fox gives a knowing nod in Mama's direction.

"Then it's obvious why you've come."

"What do you mean?"

"I know why she has come to Gilead."

Mama walks up to us. She remembers Fox from the shop. They acknowledge each other with silent glances. But Fox tells Mama, "You're looking for the little girl's family. The little girl from your school."

"Can I still find the family here?"

Fox points up towards the building. "Seventh floor."

"Do you know the apartment number?"

Fox shrugs. The apartment number, he does not know.

"Don't bother looking for a name in the lobby. It's been taken down. People are moving out... being kicked out. But you won't need it. You'll know which apartment it is when you reach the floor."

The intercom to buzz us into the building is broken, as is the lock to the entrance door. Mama and I just walk right in. The lights in the hallway are dim. The lack of light obscures scarred blue walls of peeling paint and cracked plaster. The hallway is silent, too, with a quiet that is deep and unsettling. No voices can be heard. Nor do we hear the beat of music being played behind the doors of the ground floor apartments. The only sound is the echo that seems to come from the clicking gears and creaking wheels of my bike. A building that once housed so many people shouldn't be so quiet.

Mama and I wait by the elevator. The hum of its motor breaks the silence as it begins its slow descent to us. When it arrives, the elevator is empty. Mama takes a peep inside before entering. I follow behind. Mama and I remain quiet as the elevator quivers back and forth on its way up. The elevator soon comes to a stop and the gate slides to the side. Mama pushes the door open and we walk out onto a seventh floor that is darker and bleaker than the lobby downstairs. Four lights, evenly spaced, run the length of the hallway. But only two lights, each at opposite ends, are working. The silence is troubling. I'm in the Dead Zone.

Fox is right. It is obvious which apartment belongs to the family of the little girl. A small bundle of dried dying flowers has been laid at the doorstep. Cards of sympathy have been taped to the door. I start to open up one of the cards to read. But before I can do so, Mama gently moves my hand away and closes the card. She shakes her head. "No".

Mama knocks on the door.

There is no answer. But we can hear movement inside. Slow and lazy footsteps, the sound of slippers shuffling across the floor. As the steps grow nearer, I watch Mama nervously bite her bottom lip. Soon, I can feel someone on the opposite side of the door. I can feel the presence of someone on the other side of the peephole. A lock is unfastened. Then another. The door opens up slowly, so just a sliver and a ray of light sneaks out. The door opens no further. It's held back by a thin, gold chain that looks like it could be cut by a pair of old rusty scissors. All Mama and I can see, is a lone, cold, gray eye staring at us.

"Hello," Mama says nervously. "I'm..."

"I know who you are, Teacher." The voice that slips through the crack in the door is weary. It sounds like the worn-down voice of an old woman. "You want to speak to the mother."

"Yes."

"The mother's not here."

"Where might I find her?"

"Who knows," says the old lady. "She's probably outside in the courtyard or whiling away on some bench in the school's playground... drinking... and waiting on a miracle."

Mama doesn't seem to know how to respond. To say 'thank you', doesn't seem appropriate.

The gaze from the eye watching us seems to soften for a moment. The old lady on the other side of the door says, "I'm not sure why you came to Gilead. There are no fairytale endings in this place."

Then the old lady extends a wrinkled hand through the door. Mama takes the hand and brings it close to her cheek and holds it there for a moment. The door opens slightly. I can see, just barely, the old lady's features. I notice a wisp of gray hair, and I can see—faintly—lips that are delicate, full, and soft. The old lady kisses Mama's hand, and says, "Peace be with you."

Mama and I make our way outside again. It's deathly quiet. I don't see Fox anymore. I don't know what shadow he has slipped off to hide in. I turn back and look up at the Tower of Gilead. It is clear to me now that hardly anybody lives here anymore. I can see through open windows without curtains or blinds. There is no one, just empty apartments staring back at me.

Mama tells me, "Come."

We cross the street and head toward the school's courtyard. There's a woman sitting alone on a plastic bench close to the school. She sits beneath the shade of a newly planted tree, one of four that dot the corners of the school's courtyard. To her side, are two large red doors. From the woman's vantage point, she has a near panoramic view of a barren playground. The woman sees Mama and me coming.

Mama says, "I want to speak to her alone." She tells me to stay put. "Don't ride off. Stay right where I can see you. Don't go beyond the park's front fence."

FORTY-FOUR

Hannah sees someone not unlike herself, a mother, sitting alone in a desolate schoolyard. Hannah imagines that, as with her, many people who pass by know this woman's name. They know her story. Where the two women differ, Hannah looks upon the mother whose little child is lost.

Hannah glances over to check on the Boy. She sees that he is doing as told, riding his bike a safe distance away. So, Hannah makes her way towards Princess' Mother. She has a look that is familiar to Hannah—lost, vacant eyes that stare out into the distance. Hannah knows the feeling behind this look. It does little to mask feelings of shame and disappointment. It is a mask unable to hide pain and embarrassment. But Princess' Mother is able to come out of her haze as Hannah approaches. There is a hint of recognition in her eyes. The mother offers Hannah a tired smile. She gestures for Hannah to have a seat on the bench alongside her.

"I knew it would be just a matter of time before I'd see you again," says Princess' Mother. There is neither anger nor belligerence in her voice, just weariness. The mother fixes her eyes back to the playground, and sees the Boy riding his bike. Without lifting her gaze away from him, she asks, "That's your son?"

"Yes," says Hannah.

"He's a beautiful boy. You are blessed to have him."

Hannah feels awkward but manages a nod of thanks. The moment seems to last forever as Princess' Mother watches Hannah's child ride his bike in circles. Hannah sees that he is trying to do wheelies. This makes Hannah smile. But the mother who stares out at Hannah's son does so without expression. Never taking her eyes off the boy, Princess' Mother tells Hannah, "You and your son should not have come to Gilead."

"I wanted to see you."

"Why... to say that you're sorry? It wasn't your fault."

"I was the last person to see your child. I let her go away with him."

"He always planned to take her."

"I'm not sure I understand. You knew this would happen?"

"He would sometimes joke, 'If I could only take one of you away from this godforsaken place. Who would it be?'"

Hannah feels light-headed and disoriented. She should not listen anymore. Be careful what you wish for. *The closure you seek won't be found in Gilead.*

"He should have taken me. We were supposed to have a life together away from here. Just him and me. The little girl would have been safe with my mother."

"So, that's what hurts you? That *you* were left behind."

The Princess' Mother doesn't seem to hear Hannah. "The girl shouldn't have meant anything to him. She wasn't his daughter. He was supposed to take *me* away from this place. I should have seen it coming, the buying of her affection with little gifts. I made the mistake of letting him hold her, of allowing him to rock her in his arms when she was a baby. She became his little girl... his little angel. I should have known better than to let that child come between us."

"You're not concerned about what has become of your daughter?"

"God watches over small children. The question is—'when will He watch over me? When will I get what I desire?'"

Hannah lets silence fall in the space between them. The envelope that she had been holding, drops from her lap and onto the ground. Hannah picks it up. Princess' Mother asks, "Is that for me?"

"No," says Hannah, quietly. "It is mine."

Hannah places the envelope back into her knapsack. She looks up and finds that Princess' Mother has returned her lost gaze to the desolate schoolyard. The mother's mind is elsewhere. When she speaks, it is almost as if to herself. "Every day, I come out here and I sit. People walk by and they stare. They watch me from their windows. They all know my story.

They pity me. 'There goes the mother of the little child lost.' And they think they know why I sit here. They think it's about the little girl. That I'm just waiting on her return. I don't want their pity. I don't need it. Because it's not about the little girl. I just want him to come back and take me away from here, too."

Hannah slips her knapsack back over her shoulders. She can't bring herself to look at Princess' Mother. "I shouldn't have come. I'm sorry."

"A smart person like you should have known that there's no healing in this place. Only Madness."

FORTY-FIVE

Gilead is a place of nothingness. That's the best way I can describe it. It's like a Dead Zone. It's a place of no life. The schoolyard has no swings, no slides, no sandpit—and no children. There are two rimless basketball backboards that hang battered and crooked on the wired fence that surrounds the yard. No one walks the streets here. It is a silent and lonely place.

But my eyes play tricks on me. I see a child on a bike in the distance, not far from the lot Mama and I passed by before. It's a chubby boy staring my way. I know who it is. It's Tum Tum. I shouldn't be surprised that I see him. It figures he'd be the only kid around. There's nobody to care or look after him. He's usually always in a hurry to ride up to me whenever he sees me. But Tum Tum's acting strange now. He seems to be waiting on *me* to go riding after him. He just sits there on his bike. I'm curious what's going on with him.

Mama is still talking to the lady, so she is not really paying me any mind. It's almost like me and Tum Tum are in the same boat. Two lost children out here all alone. So, I start to ride over to him. As I do, he starts to pedal away. I guess he wants me to follow him.

Tum Tum doesn't wait for me. He crosses the street on his bike and heads for the open construction lot and its mounds of dirt. Knowing Tum Tum, he's going to want to bet and see who has a better dirt bike. But Tum Tum is pedaling fast and doesn't stop to ride up any of the mounds. Tum Tum turns around and motions for me to hurry and catch up. He rides up to one of the buildings and vanishes into the dark hole of an unfinished doorway.

I reach the entrance. But I turn to look back at the school-yard. I'm far away and can't see Mama. I look up to the sky and the gray clouds have grown near black. There's a rumble of thunder somewhere not so far away. The heavens are going to open up any minute. Shoot. I need to go back. I need to be listening to Mama.

"Yo, kid, over here."

I don't get off my bike. I just stare into the empty hole that is this doorway. There is no sign of Tum Tum. There is just a voice echoing through a huge open space of pillars, coiled pipes, and wires that are hanging from an unfinished ceiling. I feel a drop of rain. Then another, and another.

"Yo, kid," says a voice again. "You better get inside. You're going to get rained on."

The rain is starting to come down harder. There's no turning back. I head inside for cover.

FORTY-SIX

Hannah swears she had just seen the Boy doing as told, riding his bike right in front of her. But now the Boy is nowhere to be seen. And the sky is opening up. It is starting to rain.

Hannah feels a strange churning in the pit of her stomach, followed by a sharp and sudden chill in the blood that runs through her veins. Hannah begins to shiver, and she begins to feel light-headed. There's a quick flash of white before her eyes. She regains sight but then has no sense of her surroundings. When her head clears, Hannah starts to walk but her first few steps are difficult, and she stumbles. Her heart begins to race. Hannah needs to take a seat, but there's no time for that. "Oh, God. My child is gone."

"Have you seen..." Hannah turns to Princess' Mother. But she has vanished. And perhaps the Boy has too. But where?

Hannah tries to think clearly, but it's a struggle. Is she even sure what the boy is wearing? Cargo shorts? An oversized blue

T-shirt two sizes too big? Black high-top sneakers? Hannah cannot say. She runs over towards the Tower of Gilead. Perhaps the Boy is waiting out the rain over there. But she quickly sees that he is not underneath the stone overhang at the building's entranceway. Hannah walks into the building to see if he is somewhere in the lobby. He is not. All she finds is a deep silence.

Hannah steps back outside into the rain and sets off along the narrow path leading away from the Tower. But Hannah feels paralyzed by the painful truth that her misguided quest to seek meaning in the troubled life of a child of Gilead may have come at the expense of losing her own child. *What kind of a mother am I?* Hannah stops at the feeble garden along this path and takes a seat on a battered bench beneath the limp branches of a dying tree. With no regard to the steady rain that falls down upon her, Hannah begins to weep.

———————

A young man stands in the shadows watching Hannah.

It is Fox. And he has been watching Hannah ever since he saw her come to Gilead with the Boy. He has kept his distance, making sure he has gone unnoticed. He watched from the darkness of a staircase when Hannah and the child spoke to the old lady. And Fox saw, too, how they were led back to the courtyard to find the little girl's mother sitting alone. Now, from the shadows of an outer stairwell leading down to the Tower's basement, Fox keeps a watchful eye on Hannah. But he doesn't see the Boy. Fox only sees Hannah weeping.

Fox has never seen a mother cry for a child before. In his world, a mother abandons her child for a five-dollar high. In Fox's world, a mother doesn't tell her child to follow their dreams. To see a mother weep for a child seems unreal to Fox.

Fox emerges from the stairwell knowing the Boy could not have gone far. Fox looks out onto a deserted street. He sees a neighborhood rib shack, a small hut-sized building located on the other side of the street. Out in front of its dilapidated doorway, crimson colored lights from neon beer signs dance in the rain's slowly forming puddles of water. Fox sees a shadow appear in the doorway. But it is the long and slender shadow of the shack's gatekeeper. Fox figures there are only so many places the Boy can be—the boarded-up store next to the rib shack, and a construction lot across the street. Fox wonders, *where can the boy be?*

FORTY-SEVEN

I follow the echo of Tum Tum's voice and ride further inside the building. It's not long until I finally see him. Tum Tum has made a make-shift ramp from a large discarded piece of broken wood and two large white barrels. Tum Tum speeds up to the ramp and soars high into the air until he lands and disappears further into the dark expanse of this huge open space.

From somewhere deep in the darkness, I hear Tum Tum say, "I bet you can't leap as far as me."

I should know better than to get caught up in his silly challenges, but I go for it. I pedal fast up to the ramp and fly high into the sky. As I land, I see a hand reach out from the shadows with a long rod and catch my bike's front wheel. I flip over the handlebars head-first and tumble hard, rolling end-over-end along the ground. I don't know how long I lay there. I'm not sure if anything is broken. I can feel the skin burning on my hands and knees. They are scraped really bad. I'm too weak to look down, but I can feel blood gliding down my elbows, my shoulder, and my knees. Suddenly, I feel two hands lift me roughly up onto my feet. Then there's a swift punch to my stomach. I double over and I fall back to the ground. Then I hear a voice. Not a kid's voice, but one that is as deep and hard as that of a grown man. "Sit him up."

"Oh, oh, oh... OK." That voice I know. It's Tum Tum.

Everything is blurry. Tum Tum props me up. I am able to make him out as he leans over and gives me quick look-over. Tum Tum glances towards a dark shadow. I follow his nervous eyes, and soon I hear steps approaching from the dark space. Appearing out of the black hole is someone I have never seen before. My eyes struggle to bring into focus a scrawny-looking teenager, who is wearing a dark blue, long-sleeved T-shirt that's about three sizes too big for him, and a pair of sagging jeans. At first glance, he doesn't look like someone to fear. But then he leans closer and brings his face close to mine. He looks me up and down with vacant black eyes. And then there's that scar that runs deep and jagged across his right cheek. It's Tum Tum's brother, Scarface.

"Give it to me," he says.

I might be a bit dazed and a little out of it, but I know what he wants. Tum Tum told him about the anklet. They're convinced that it's worth a lot of money. But I'm not giving it to them. I act like I don't understand what he's asking me. I give a blank look and say, "Huh?"

"That jewelry with the diamonds," says Tum Tum, kind of scared. "My brother wants it."

I'm still feeling a little groggy, but I manage to tell him, "I don't..."

Before I can finish answering, Scarface slaps me hard.

Scarface then asks, "Do you know me?"

"Yes, I know you."

"Do you fear me?"

I know the answer he wants to hear. He won't get it out of me. "I don't fear you. I don't fear nobody."

Scarface slaps me again, right upside my ear. It rings badly, but I manage to hear him say, "Tough talk from a mama's boy. Tum Tum has told me about you. Your mama ain't here to save you."

"Yo, kid, just give it to him."

"I'm telling you, I don't have it."

Scarface orders Tum Tum to steady me on my feet. He hits me in my stomach. I feel the wind get knocked out of me. It feels like I'm going to die. I don't put up any fight as he begins rifling through my pockets. He goes into my left and right pockets and pulls out nothing but some crusty pieces of old napkins rolled up into little small balls.

"Where is it?!!?"

Scarface raises his hand and is about to hit me again. But I don't make it so easy. Before his fist comes down on me, I wiggle free. I start to run, but I stumble and fall. Tum Tum grabs hold of me from behind again. He reaches for my back pocket and yanks out the small candy box. Scarface looks at the box with disgust. Scarface takes the candy box he's holding and throws it at me. It hits me in the eye and falls to the ground. The anklet falls out.

Tum Tum can't believe it. "Oh, shit!"

Scarface walks over to the anklet and kneels down to pick it up. He remains kneeling while he studies the diamonds closely. He doesn't bother reading the words inscribed on the anklet. Scarface looks up at me. "Son of a bitch, you had it all the time. I guess you did mean it when you said you didn't fear me. Otherwise, you wouldn't have lied."

Scarface picks up the steel rod lying on the ground. Tum Tum still has a hold of me, but his voice begins to quiver when he asks, "Wha... What are you doing?"

"I'm going to make this mama's boy fear me."

Scarface slowly walks up to me with the rod firmly in his hand. He expects me to cry and beg. He expects me to give up. *OK. OK, Scarface, you want it. Come closer.* Then out of the blue, I spit in his face and directly into his eye.

My defiance has blinded him. And for a brief second, Scarface lowers the rod. "You will learn to respect me, little boy."

Scarface raises the rod and is about to bring it down on my head, when a voice calls out calmly from somewhere deep in the shadows. "I don't think so."

Fox steps from the darkness and into a strand of light that slips in through a small opening in the wall. He asks, "Is there a problem?"

Scarface tries to show he's not afraid of Fox. But I can see a slight tremble in his hand, as he tries to steady his grip of the rod. He has yet to lower it. "This doesn't concern you, Fox."

"I'm making it my concern." Fox lifts up his shirt, revealing a gun tucked away in his waistband. "So, I'll ask again: is there a problem?"

Scarface doesn't lower the steel rod. Fox calmly places his hand on his pistol. He doesn't even draw it. Fox tells Scarface, "If anybody knows about fear, it's you. Don't be stupid. You know I'll take you out and think nothing of it."

Scarface locks eyes with me. He finally lowers the steel rod and tosses it away. Fox looks over at Tum Tum. He doesn't say anything. Tum Tum loosens his grip and I fall to my hands and knees. Then I hear Fox say, "Give it back."

I look up at Scarface, and his eyes are narrow as he glares at me. He slowly releases the anklet and lets it fall by my hand.

Then Fox says, "Good."

Scarface says nothing. He looks over to Tum Tum. "Let's get out of here."

Tum Tum let's go of me, and I drop to the cold concrete. I hear Tum Tum's and Scarface's footsteps as they walk away. They are soon replaced by Fox's steps, as he walks towards me. Fox kneels beside me and picks up the anklet. Fox looks at the diamonds. Then he plays with it in his hand and takes the time to read the inscribed words. Fox hands it back to me. Then, suddenly, he just picks me up, slings me over his shoulder, and carries me out of this dark pit.

CHAPTER

FORTY-EIGHT

A light rain falls after a passing storm. A mother weeps for her lost child.

Fox carries the Boy in the hollow of one arm. Fox totes the Boy's bike with his other hand. Hannah sprints over to the young man. He gently lowers the Boy into her arms. Hannah falls to her knees at the feet of this stranger, cradling her son in her arms. Hannah kisses the Boy and squeezes him tight in her arms. The Boy manages to look up and see his mother crying.

"I'm sorry, Mama... I'm sorry, Mama..."

Hannah looks up at the young man who brought back her son. Fox gazes down at Hannah impassively but with a hint of understanding in his eyes. Hannah reaches for his hand and holds it close to her. "Thank you," she says to this stranger. "Thank you." Hannah turns her attention back to the Boy and draws him near. She leans closer to make out what he is saying to her. "You were right... never stray off the path. You were right, Mama..."

Hannah notices that the Boy is holding tightly onto something in his hand. She unfurls his fist and sees a beautiful anklet. The Boys says, "This belongs to you now, Mama. It's yours. It found you."

Hannah raises the anklet and studies the shiny diamonds. She turns it over gently in her hands. Hannah notices the inscription on the anklet. Hannah reads the words. *God Is.*

Hannah manages a soft smile, and tells the Boy, "Indeed, *God is.*"

FORTY-NINE

"My grace is sufficient for you..."
—2 Corinthians 12:9

I refuse to make things up just so that I can give meaning to that which is beyond my understanding. I won't pacify myself and pretend to always know the Truth.

One mother asks another, "Why is my child lost, but yours is out of harm's way?" *I don't know, but I am thankful.*

You ask me, "Why was a stranger there for me in time of threat and danger?" *I don't know, but I am thankful.*

God Is... what? I'm not sure I can answer that for you. You might say God Is... Unexplainable. God Is... Real. God is... Silence. The best answer for me is, God Is... Grace. I don't know. You have to complete it with a word of your choosing. Pick something that works best for you. Whatever you choose, it will hold the Truth.

FIFTY

It's past one o'clock in the morning. The old candy shop is closed. Its security gate has been lowered shut, so the Old Man walks around to the back alley. It is a narrow lane, cluttered with dumpsters, discarded boxes, and bags of trash. The backdoor to the old shop lies just beyond a ten-foot high locked fence. The Old Man shakes a steel chain that is coiled around the iron gate. He gets the attention of a shadowy figure standing in the candy shop's rear doorway. The man named Me-Too hears the rattle of the chain, and steps out of the shadows. Me-Too says nothing as he walks over to the fence. He unfastens the chain. The Old Man steps through the gate, then stops to watch Me-Too lock it behind them. Me-Too points towards the backdoor and says, "Go. He's expecting you."

The Old Man steps inside the shop. The backroom parlor is dark and empty of people except for the Merchant, who sits waiting at the poker table. Me-Too walks over to the Old

Man and gets ready to frisk him. The Old Man reaches into his jacket's breast pocket, pulls out a white envelope, and sticks his hands up in surrender.

The Merchant waves Me-Too off.

"He's just a sorry old man. Leave him."

The Merchant points to an empty seat opposite him at the table. The Old Man walks over, pulls out a chair, and takes a seat. He glances behind and watches Me-Too lock the back-door. The big man places the key chain around his neck and remains standing by the door.

"Well..." says the Merchant. He lets the rest of his question go unspoken.

The Old Man reaches inside the breast pocket of his windbreaker, and takes out a white letter-sized envelope. He places it on the table, but keeps his hand on it. He doesn't pass it over to The Merchant. "What's inside this envelope is how much your silence is worth to me. When I give it to you, our business will be done for good."

The Merchant says nothing. He is waiting for the Old Man pass it over to him.

The Old Man smiles and laughs softly. "You know, I learned long time ago how to deal with people like you... and the Kid. Some believe the way to deal with you is to pacify you. Those people will sell you lies. You may have had a chance if someone told you the truth a long time ago. Someone should have told you that the path you're on is for cowards, and for fools. You would have seen the truth about yourself and perhaps would have tried to do something meaningful with your life."

"You hear this motherfucker, Me-Too?"

Me-Too nods and places his hand on the 9 mm pistol tucked in his waistband.

The Old Man shakes his head and mocks them both with a smile. "I imagine you had a mama who wondered, 'What am I going to do with my boy?' And she was given a one-word answer, 'Love. Just love him with all your heart and soul.' But she'd say, 'That would require too much effort. I got my own life to live.' You became an unloved child who would grow up to be a menace to those who just want to live quietly.

"And that's unfortunate, because every now and then, someone like you and the Kid cross paths with someone like me. I'm not here to pacify you like others have done all your life. I'm not scared of what your ignorance and your greed can do to me. People like you and the Kid have no power over me. In reality, my man, it's the other way around. I have power over you. I merely take you out and move on my way."

The Merchant gives a slow, mocking applause. He is laughing at the Old Man. "You stay up all night writing that." The Merchant reaches from under the table and reveals his 9 mm gun. He calmly places it front of himself on the table and rests his hands on it. "You got it wrong, Old Man. I am enlightened. Those with true wisdom know that life is meaningless. Get what you can now. Your words are nothing more than a lot of sound and fury spoken by an old fool. Your words, your life, mean nothing. All that matters is that you are here at my table with the money I told you to bring. And you'll be moving on, only if I see fit."

The sight of the gun doesn't alarm the Old Man. He remains unfazed. The Old Man tells the Merchant, "No, I'll be leaving right out that door over there when I say so. Like a shadow, like I was never here. And I'll be leaving shortly after we finish our business here." The Old Man taps the envelope. "I'm only here because I can engage in games. Here is what the story and its silence is worth."

The Old Man slides the envelope over to the Merchant. The Merchant studies the envelope for a moment. Then he looks over at the Old Man. He can't help but offer up a sly, knowing smile. The Merchant finally picks up the envelope and opens it.

The envelope is empty.

With an intense glare, the Old Man locks eyes with The Merchant. "How could I pay you for a story whose ending you didn't know? You claim to like stories. Mine is about a soldier who easily found his prey and took him on a long ride far, far from this place. It was a long, quiet ride. Not a word was spoken. The soldier kept wondering, 'Why was this kid so special? Why did this Merchant claim him like a son?' You know that to be a soldier you have to be a hunter. This soldier searched out answers. He heard the rumors about a woman, the Kid's mother. Did you love her? Are you capable of that? And when the Kid's mother passed on, was she hopped up on some bad drugs you gave her by mistake? The soldier heard of a promise this Boss Man made that he would always protect the Kid. But you did nothing more than corrupt him.

"The soldier couldn't give all this too much thought because all he heard during that long drive was the whimpering of the

Kid from the back seat. This boy realized that his life was about to end. And so, this soldier eventually stopped this car in some outback forest far, far from The City. And he and the Kid went for a walk. The Kid didn't make a move to run because the soldier had a pistol aimed dead at him. It was the Kid's own pistol.

"The soldier and Kid came to a clearing where up ahead there was a lone train track that cut its way along a dark green hillside. The soldier told the Kid, 'Drop to your knees, boy.' The Kid did as he was told. And he began to weep.

"The old soldier walked up to the Kid and placed the gun against the back of the Kid's head, and said to him, 'Deny him.'

"The Kid was confused. 'I don't understand.'

"The soldier said again, 'Deny the man who is like a father to you. Tell me, that he no longer means anything to you.'

"The soldier placed the gun more firmly against the back of his head. 'I will help you. Answer me, "Do you know him?"'

"And the Kid who cared about nothing else except his own little life, gave the only answer he could, 'No. I don't know him. He is nothing to me.' And the Kid began to weep some more.

"The soldier lowered the gun and he pulled out, believe it or not, an envelope and dropped it in front of the boy. 'Take it,' he said. The Kid didn't know what to do. So, the soldier said, 'Take the money inside. The passport and new I.D. Walk along those tracks until you come to a station. Get on the next train and go away somewhere far from here. Don't ever come back to The City. If you return, I will know that you're not a man of your word.'

"And the Kid asked, 'If I am not a man of my word?'

"'You will die again, this time for real.

"And so the Kid allowed himself to be bought off. He took the money and denied you. Never to be heard from again. And that is how the story truly ends. A proud woman told me when the time came, I was to return and confront the true evil behind the dishonoring of her child. This woman told me to come here in her name, and to let you know, 'You don't win'."

There is a deep silence in the room. The Merchant tightens his grip on the 9 mm, preparing to take aim at the Old Man. But all of a sudden there is a click. The Old Man reaches out from beneath the table, and with his switchblade, slices the Merchant's hand that's resting on the gun. The Old Man swipes the gun, gets a hold of it firmly and confidently fires a shot at the Merchant, sending him tumbling backwards out of his chair. Me-Too is shocked as he fumbles with his aim. The Old Man takes a calm and steady aim at Me-Too and fires two shots. He strikes Me-Too between his upper chest and shoulder. Me-Too drops his gun and falls in a heap in the doorway.

The Old Man remains seated. He has fired three shots without blinking an eye. There is silence all around him. He takes out a handkerchief and wipes the handle of the gun. He takes out a pair of leather gloves and puts them on. Suddenly, the silence is broken by a muted wail from the shadows.

"God, help me... God... help me..."

The Old Man calmly pushes himself back from the table, and walks over to the voice. It is Me-Too. "Oh God, help me..."

The Old Man sees Me-Too's fallen gun lying by his side. The Old calmly places his foot on it, then kicks it away. With the gun he his holding, the Old Man takes aim at Me-Too.

"God... God help me... help me..."

The Old Man asks, "Do you know me?"

"Please... God... help... help..."

The plea fades away into the void. The Old Man lowers his pistol and walks over to The Merchant who lies gravely wounded. The Merchant looks up at the Old Man wearily but defiantly, and without fear. The Old Man locks eyes with him. He raises his gun and points it at The Merchant. No words are spoken

Two shots ring out in the night.

FIFTY-ONE

M ama has a story to share.

An outsider finds himself walking along the Road Less Traveled.
He's a craftsman, a carpenter by trade. He spends his days and
nights cutting and shaping the beams of wood that support the
path of the subway tracks that snake their way through The
City. And now, he emerges from the tunnel that twists and
bends beneath the Road Less Traveled. He exits the train station
alone. He seeks a moment of rest and a meal, before heading
back to work.

But the Carpenter has gotten himself turned around. He
meant to exit at the other end of the station through the gate that
would have left him closer to that place called The Madness. It is a
few minutes before midnight, the streets are dark and desolate and
there is no late-night eatery in sight.

The Carpenter is lost.

He can very well return to the subway's pit and retrace his steps. But instead, he tells himself to just walk along the same path above ground under the light of a full moon. There is a playground up ahead. Most would feel compelled to cross over to the other side of the street believing that it's never safe to walk past an empty schoolyard late at night. There's no telling what may lurk in the shadows. But the Carpenter does not yield to such fear. He continues along the path.

The Carpenter walks past the schoolyard and sees a rustling in the shadows beneath the massive oak tree at the center of the park. He sees a body huddled, curled in a ball, shivering and weeping. The Carpenter walks over to the body and kneels down beside it. He sees a young girl, probably eighteen years of age, but no older than twenty. She has been badly beaten.

Weakly, she says, "Help me, please. Help me."

The Carpenter takes her hand and holds it. He doesn't squeeze hard, nor does he take her hand roughly. The Carpenter says to the young girl, "Shhh, don't be afraid."

"Look what's been done to me. No one would stop and help me. You're the only one. Who would do such a thing? What kind of world is this? The Madness." The young girl continues to weep softly. "Your name? Tell me your name?"

The Carpenter takes a single finger and gently traces it along her brow and then along the young girl's eyelid, wiping away the dirt and bloodied hair that blocks her vision. His touch is gentle. "Joshua. My name is Joshua."

Joshua... my name is Joshua. Now that you know my story, you may now know my name. My name is Joshua.

FIFTY-TWO

Hannah's child wakes up and it's a new day. His scars from Gilead are not going away anytime soon. He knows he'll be cooped up in the house for a little while. But that's OK. He knows that he will heal.

Hannah calls for him to come down to the basement apartment. The Boy runs to her voice and finds her standing in the open doorway of the Old Man's apartment.

"He's gone."

These words hold no surprise. Hannah motions for the Boy to come closer and invites him to enter the studio apartment. He steps into a large room bathed in sunlight. The apartment is spotless. The bed is freshly made, military grade with the linen razor-sharp and tucked in tight along all sides.

"Have a look on the table," says Hannah.

A small worktable and chair are set against a rectangular wall that divides two windows that look out ground level to the street outside. Atop the table is a small ivory-colored note card.

Hannah says, "Go on. You can read it."

I believe in family. That's why I came back... to feel like a part of a family again. But the bonds that keep family strong and safe must be pure. They must be rooted in honesty and in truth. They can't be obscured by secrets or by unspoken truths, or half-truths. In a family, people must be honest about who they are. I'm a selfish old man incapable of sharing myself completely and honestly. And that is why I must go.

I want you to know this... you and the boy are special to me. And I want you to know that you are loved.

The Boy stops reading. He takes a look to see if there is more written on the other side. It is blank.

"There's nothing more needed. It says it all."

The Boy says nothing at first. For a moment, he considers what his mother has said, perhaps wondering about the fairness of it all because finally he says, "How will the Old Man ever know that we love him too?"

FIFTY-THREE

The Quiet Hour is like it once was. Just Mama and me alone again, sitting in different parts of the living room with our thoughts. Mama has her artist sketch pad in her lap. She's sitting on the windowsill. I have *Wolf and Boy* in my lap but have yet to open it. I tell Mama, "I never got a chance to tell the Old Man the end of this story."

"You can tell me," says Mama, with a soft smile. "Because a story told must have an ending."

———

It is said the boy never returned to the life he had known in the village. No one there was really sure of his fate. No one ever went looking. But there is one tale, told by a brave hunter, who became lost after chasing a large deer up the mountain one day. When he returned, he told a wild and unbelievable story of a boy and a wolf lying asleep together under a tree some distance away. But as he made his way, thrashing and crashing through the forest to where he thought he would rescue the lad, he became lost and could neither see nor find them. And so, he returned to his safe villager's life, speaking in hushed tones of his brief glimpse of a different life he would never understand. People listened to his story, told over and over again until the words were worn. And as the long years passed, some who listened laughed. Some wept quietly. A few crossed themselves in disgust. And, once and again, some few took heart and would lie awake at night listening with hope to the strange and wolfish duet, sung high upon a distant peak in the silver moonlight.

FIFTY-FOUR

The people in church exalt as the choir sings.

The LORD is my shepherd;
I shall not want.
He maketh me to lie down in green pastures:
He leadeth me beside the still waters.
He restoreth my soul;
And He leadeth me into the path of righteousness
for His name's sake.
Yea, though I walk through the valley in the shadow of death,
I will fear no evil:
For thou art with me;
thy rod and thy staff, they comfort me.
Thou preparest a table before me
in the presence of mine enemies;
Thou anointest my head with oil;

my cup runneth over.
Surely goodness and mercy shall follow me all the days of my life;
and I shall dwell in the house of the LORD
forever and ever and ever...
and I shall dwell in the house of the LORD
and I shall dwell in the house of the LORD... forever (My King)
and I shall dwell in the house of the LORD, forever (My Master)
and I shall dwell in the house of the LORD... forever
and I shall dwell in the house of the LORD... forever
and I shall dwell in the house of the LORD... forever
and I shall dwell in the house of the LORD... forever
forever...
forever...
forever...

The final chorus fades away, yet Pastor remains seated. He makes no movement from his chair. He doesn't step towards the pulpit and engage in his usual small talk about the choir's performance. Instead, Pastor remains motionless with his eyes closed. Anxiety begins to grow in his church. People start to shift uneasily in the pews.

But Pastor finally speaks, though it's almost in a whisper. It's almost as though he is speaking to himself. The little microphone attached to his jacket's lapel barely picks up Pastor saying, "Jesus is nice. And He wants us to be nice, too."

Pastor rises from his seat and slowly walks up to the dais. Again, he repeats almost wearily, but now loud enough for all to hear, "Jesus is nice. And He wants us to be nice, too."

He pauses for a moment to straighten a few papers at the pulpit. "That's what the church's message has become. A simple and easily digestible message for a child, or worse, an adult who thinks like a child. A little boy asked me recently, 'My mother is in pain. Can you say something for her? A word that will help her understand?' I look around now, and I don't see the boy and his mother sitting here amongst you. And I'm saddened. Because I know his mama. I know her story. I know her pain. She wants to come to a place where she'll hear a message that holds power. She wants a message of Truth. The mother seeks wisdom. A word based on wisdom will ease her pain. Jesus is nice and He wants us to be nice, too. That's not a message of wisdom. There is so much to this faith. There is so much to His teachings. And it's not about being nice.

"Jesus is nice. And He wants us to be nice, too. It's a message rooted in what we think it means to have the correct beliefs. We treat our faith as though we are signing a contract where we agree to follow a strict set of rules. It's a message for those who want something easy to manage. It's for juvenile thinkers who want a message of what to eat and not eat, what to wear and not wear. They want a message that tells them who they should allow into your home and who they should not. A message that answers the question: Who is my neighbor?

"But let me be honest with you. A real seeker of truth asks, 'what did Jesus teach?' The true seeker is not so much concerned about where in the history books one finds proof of His existence. Rather, this seeker of truth wants to know, 'how do we get inside the mind of Jesus and view our place in the world through His eyes?' The true seeker wants to know, 'how do we feel through His heart?'

"'Who do you say I am?' This is something Jesus asks over and over again in the Gospels. What He's really asking is, 'who or what in *you* recognizes me? Do you know me?'

"To answer this question requires wisdom. And when you're about the wisdom of Jesus Christ, it's not about the correct beliefs. It's about the correct practices.

"How do we die before we die? How do we love our neighbors as we love ourselves? How do we connect that which we believe into what we can actually live? These are profound questions. But we think, if we *say* we believe it, or if we know what page to flip to in the Bible to where it's written... or if we preach it... that we can just do it.

"But it's not possible.

"That is, not until we go beyond the mind. To do so, we must focus on the path that seeks to answer, 'how is Jesus like us? How is that what He did, something that we can do ourselves.' This is a different teaching from those that teach that Christ is different from us, belonging to a higher order of being.

"As I am, you, too, can and must become. I will be here to help you, but you must do the work yourself."

———— ◡ ————

There was a scholar of the law who stood up to test Jesus, and said, "Teacher, what must I do to inherit eternal life?"

Jesus said to him, **"What is written in the law? How do you read it?"** *The scholar said in reply, "You shall love the Lord, your God, with all your heart, with all your being, with all your strength, and with all your mind, and your neighbor as yourself."*

Since the Lawyer cited the Law, Jesus replied to him, **"You have answered correctly; do this and you will live."** *But the Lawyer, desiring to justify himself, said to Jesus, "And who is my neighbor?"*

"A man was going down from Jerusalem to Jericho, and he fell among robbers, who stripped him and beat him and departed, leaving him half-dead. Now, by chance, a priest was going down that road, and when he saw him, he passed by on the other side. So, likewise a Levite, when he came to the place and saw him, passed by on the other side. But a Samaritan, as he journeyed, came to where he was, and when he saw him, he had compassion. He went to him and bound up his wounds, pouring on oil and wine. Then he set him on his own animal and brought him to an inn and took care of him. And the next day, he took out two denarii and gave them to the innkeeper, saying, 'Take care of him, and whatever more you spend, I will repay you when I come back.' Which of these three, do you think, proved to be a neighbor to the man who fell among the robbers?" *He said,* **"The one who showed him mercy."** *And Jesus said to him,* **"You go, and do likewise."**

"'What can I, myself, do to obtain eternal life?'" This is what the Lawyer asks at the beginning of this parable. But the Lawyer should know that we are unable to save ourselves. The Lawyer believes that eternal life is in his power. This man of law does not seem to understand salvation and the need for grace.

"In this passage, we hear Jesus ask, *'what is written in the Law?'* And what does the Lawyer do? He quotes the Law, which is correct: 'Love the Lord, your God, with all your heart, with all your being, with all your strength, and with all your mind, and your neighbor as yourself.' But the Lawyer is wrong to believe that upholding the Law is something within his power. The Lawyer is taking the call to love God with his whole heart, mind, and strength, lightly. This should not be some token gesture. If we're honest, we know that we do not love God this way. We're more concerned with serving our own needs first. The world's needs come next. And then, from whatever is left over, we give a few crumbs to God. We'll pray, if we have time at the end of our busy day at work. We'll read our Bible, if it doesn't interfere with watching the game. We'll throw a couple of dollars in the collection plate, after we pay our rent. We'll follow the teachings of God, so long as it doesn't interfere with our politics or worldview. God always gets the scraps. The Lawyer should know that, by ourselves, we can't pull off loving God with our whole heart, mind, and strength. To think that we can even come close is crazy.

"'And who is my neighbor?'

"The Lawyer wants to keep the meaning of 'neighbor' easily definable. If this world is filled with all his neighbors, there's no way he can pull this off. The Lawyer wants to dumb down the meaning of being a neighbor because this is what the flesh does: we praise God's laws but don't take them seriously. The Lawyer wants to haggle over a precise definition of 'neighbor' and keep that category as small and exclusive as possible. He has to do this because he wants to adhere to the Law, but do so on his own, by his own merit and power.

"A Jesus who is nice, and who wants us to be nice too, would allow you to live in your own fantasy. But Jesus does not play nice, and that is why He tells the Lawyer the story of the Samaritan.

"The Jesus who tells this parable is not nice and will not offer a simplistic definition of who is a neighbor. You see, the priest and the Levite refused to help the victim by the roadside. Maybe they were scared, because to touch this man would make them unclean for the Temple. They symbolize the human belief that God can be bought off by religious observance. If I go to Church, pay tithes, say a few prayers, sing along with the choir, I can convince myself that I am righteous and have met all my duties.

"We live in a time when God's providence has been replaced by the nature of progress. People now believe that we don't need God to be moral.

"When you pat yourself on the back and claim you're being righteous, it becomes easy to walk past the homeless. It becomes easy to turn a blind eye to evil and remain silent. You tell yourself God is OK with this because at least you were in church on Sunday. But Jesus is not impressed. He is saying that we can't buy God off. Going to Church, financially supporting the Word of God, praying, these things do not represent the end of faith. They are just the beginning. Let's be honest, if you really sit in the pews each Sunday, and really feel the Word, then you cannot disregard the homeless, you cannot ignore injustice, nor tolerate evil and remain silent.

"Morality for us, Christians, should not be about convenience. If you are a truly moral person, you don't just help the people you like. You don't only forgive people that you like or be nice to only people that you like.

"Jesus is nice. And he wants us to be nice too. If I was to preach that sort of message, I would finish reading this parable and then tell you to go out and live like the good Samaritan. Go forth and carry some extra money in your pocket and have some resources so you can help those in need. But that's not the point of the story. I don't want you to be biblically uneducated. I don't want to be a pastor that tells you to apply Scripture to your life. That's not the proper interpretation. I wouldn't be getting you to understand what the passage is meant to teach. You wouldn't be on the path of wisdom.

"The lesson is... we can't obey the law. We can't follow the two great commandments to love the Lord with all our heart, soul, mind, and strength; and love thy neighbor as you love yourself. We fall short. So, in the end we can't justify ourselves. But it's through grace that we are justified. God wants us to rest in the truth that it is by faith and through grace... by His love... that we are justified.

"Still, I know I'll be asked, 'Who is my neighbor?' And I'll say to you, 'Your neighbor... is those who you love.'

"But understand this, Jesus is not redefining the definition of one's neighbor in this parable. He's redefining love. What it means to love somebody."

FIFTY-FIVE

Any story told should have an ending... isn't that what Mama says? I owe you an ending for you having taken the time to journey with me. It's only fair. And so, I will tell you my ending as, well... a story.

Imagine... A Sunday, late morning, a mother and son make their way along the Road Less Traveled. They are on their way to church for the first time in a little while. The sun hangs high in the sky, a perfect circle of fire ignited to illuminate all that is beautiful in the world.

Imagine, too, at the same time, in a place far away from The City, somewhere in the southern low country, and under the same vibrant sun, an old man steps out onto his porch. He takes a long look out onto the open fields that surround his home.

Back in The City, a young man emerges from the Tower of Gilead. A large green duffel bag is slung tight over his shoulder.

The young man looks back at the courtyard of Gilead, a place of broken homes and dreams, where too many children, like a young boy and his older brother, will wake up unloved. The young man walks through The Madness, past the old candy shop, now boarded and shuttered. Closed for good. It is believed the young man is off to be a soldier. He is leaving The City behind, never to return.

And along the Road Less Traveled, the little boy and his mother pause at a playground. The park is devoid of any children. Nevertheless, the mother tells her child, "We're early, go play."

The boy darts over to the swings and, in no time, is flying high and free. He is alone, but he is happy. The boy wonders whatever became of the pretty girl who flew high and free alongside him. Maybe she was just a dream.

Imagine a mother easing back into her seat on a park bench. She fiddles with an ankle bracelet that once belonged to a child. It's been adjusted to fit her just right. It belongs to her now.

God is... Peace

God is... Grace

Imagine, at this moment, back in the southern low country, the old man rings a bell on his front porch. He does so with no emotion. Children skip and dance from the thicket of trees just off on the horizon. The old man stares at them impassively. He takes a seat on his porch and watches the children hop across the stream that runs deep out in back of his home. The children laugh and are filled with joy as they race towards Hannah's open field to play.

And imagine, too, that the echo of the old man's bell reaches The City. A mother hears its chime in the distance and takes a long, inquisitive gaze down the path of the Road Less Traveled. She smiles. The mother waves her hand to get her child's attention. The boy calls out to the mother, "Do we have to go?"

"No, there's still time before church."

Instead, she motions for him to take a look at what she sees—a group of joyful children, sprinting up the block, towards the park. A little boy smiles.

At last they come.

Imagine that.

FIFTY-SIX

"Make it your ambition to live a quiet life..."
—1 Thessalonians 4:11

Dusk settles in slowly, as the last remaining rays of sunlight find protection behind soft gray clouds. The Old Man sits on a battered chair on the front porch. He rocks back and forth and watches the last of the children at play in the open field of Hannah's. They soon begin to make their way home, hopping across the stream that flows unbroken. As the children become no more than little specks of mist on the horizon, the Old Man notices a little girl. The pretty girl is no older than eight. Her skin is chestnut, and she has raven-colored hair that is vibrant and untamed. The Old Man rises out of his seat and anchors his attention on the little girl as she sprints towards the stream. The child pauses at the water's edge and turns around to look back at the store. The pretty girl smiles and waves at the Old Man. Then, without a moment's hesitation, she hops across the stream and disappears into the thick brush on the other side.

The Old Man is pleased. The time has now come to go inside Hannah's and close up shop for the day. His work is done. The children are safe and out of harm's way. All is right with the world.

Let it be so.

ABOUT THE AUTHOR

Douglas S. Reed is an educator and author of the novel *Garden's Corner*. He holds a Bachelor of Science degree in Communications Management from Syracuse University and a Master of Science degree in Primary Education from Lehman College.

Formerly a resident of New York City and an elementary school teacher at Public School 62 (Bronx, NY), Douglas S. Reed currently teaches at Elliot Primary School and is the Founder & Head Coach of Team Hurricane Basketball Academy. When away from the classroom and the basketball court, you'll find the author living quietly and peacefully on the beautiful island of Bermuda with his wife, Lisa and stepchildren Jalen and Mia.